GAME FOR SEDUCTION

GAME FOR SEDUCTION

Bella Andre

Pocket Books

NEW YORK   LONDON   TORONTO   SYDNEY

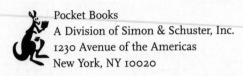
Pocket Books
A Division of Simon & Schuster, Inc.
1230 Avenue of the Americas
New York, NY 10020

First Pocket Books trade paperback edition September 2008

POCKET and colophon are registered trademarks of Simon &
Schuster, Inc.

For information about special discounts for bulk purchases,
please contact Simon & Schuster Special Sales at 1-800-456-6798
or business@simonandschuster.com.

Designed by Marie d'Augustine

Manufactured in the United States of America

10   9   8   7   6   5   4   3

Library of Congress Cataloging-in-Publication Data

Andre, Bella.
    Game for seduction / Bella Andre.—1st Pocket Books trade pbk. ed.
        p. cm.
ISBN-13: 978-1-4165-5852-1 (trade pbk.)
ISBN-10:   1-4165-5852-7 (trade pbk.)
1. Football players—Fiction. I. Title.
PS3601.N5495G38 2008
813'.6—dc22

For my parents, Louisa and Alvin, and my mother-in-law, Elaine. The hours you spend with my children make for happy grandkids . . . and finished books.

ACKNOWLEDGMENTS

Jami Alden, Monica McCarty, Anne Mallory, and Barbara Freethy pulled out all the stops to help me with this bad boy, even though they were deeply entrenched in their own books and deadlines. Thank you so much, ladies! Dave McCarty and Anton Rabushka also came through for me in a huge way.

Thank you to Carol Culver, Candice Hern, Veronica Wolff, Kate Moore, and Kalen Hughes for the endless "What should I write now?" brainstorming at the RWA national conference; to my agent, Jessica Faust, for constant support, endless encouragement, and her encyclopedic football knowledge; to my editor, Micki Nuding, for making my books shine; to my sister-in-law, Kathy, who said the two words that got this story finally rolling; and, again, to Gary Tabke for some crucial last-minute help.

Last, but not least, huge thanks to everyone at Pocket Books for putting such great covers on my books and getting them in front of so many readers.

Once a bad boy . . . always a bad boy.

CHAPTER ONE

Dominic DiMarco is seriously hot," the makeup artist said, fanning herself.

Melissa McKnight kept her eyes trained on her BlackBerry, even though she was dying for another mouthwatering look at Dominic's hard, tanned chest. As the representative for the McKnight Sports Agency, which her father owned, she wasn't there to ogle one of its clients. Assisting pro-football players during photo shoots and charity events was her job. Just because Dominic was totally drool-worthy didn't mean she could lose her head over him in public.

Only in private.

The middle-aged woman raised her voice. "You're nuts for doing email while that man has his shirt off. When are you going to get the chance to be this close to a chest that beautiful again?"

Melissa stopped typing and looked up with a polite smile. "Everyone at the McKnight Agency is very proud of what Dominic has achieved."

She'd spent a decade concealing her lust for him. That morning she'd woken up from a lovely dream in which Dominic had been doing wonderful things to her with his mouth, his amazingly strong hands, and the thick bulge between his legs, which she tried not to stare at every Sunday when he suited up for a game. She was pretty sure she failed every time.

"I couldn't care less about football," the makeup artist said, her voice too loud for Melissa's comfort. "But that man has got amazing abs. And I'll bet you can bounce a quarter off his ass."

The photographer called for some quick touch-ups to Dominic's hair, and the chatty makeup artist ran over to dust some powder on his torso. Melissa—and every other woman in the room—knew Dominic didn't really need powder to cut the shine on his perfect skin: It was simply the woman's excuse to touch him.

A photo of Dominic wearing nothing but well-worn jeans and a smile was enough to melt even the coldest woman's heart . . . and empty her pocketbook. As one of the offensive stars of the San Francisco Outlaws, Dominic was a highlight-reel favorite every Sunday when Americans were glued to their flat-screen TVs. His powerful sex appeal was the reason Melissa had been able to negotiate a $2 million endorsement fee with Levi-Strauss & Co.

Growing up in the football business, Melissa had seen plenty of impressive physiques. Great abs, tight butts, and broad shoulders were a given. But on Dominic, the standard ten had been turned up to eleven. His six-pack abs looked like they'd been painted on by a makeup artist; every time he moved, deep hollows crisscrossed his hard stomach. His wide shoulders and muscular back were a work of art, and the way the sinews and tendons of his triceps and biceps played and gave as he moved made her breath come a little too fast.

Watching him from across the room, the years fell away and she was seventeen all over again.

Every Christmas, Melissa's father invited his top clients and their wives and girlfriends over to their house. Melissa usually hid in her bedroom and read until everyone had gone home, but this year Dominic DiMarco was a new McKnight Agency client, and she couldn't resist spying on him in the living room through the pass-through counter in the kitchen.

She'd nursed a wicked crush on Dominic ever since she'd been lucky enough to tag along with her father to a University of Miami game, where Dominic had been a record-breaking wide receiver. Chills had run up and down her spine as he ran out onto the field, even though it had been a warm, sunny day. Cheerleaders kicked as high as they could and the college girls cheered wildly in their skimpiest tank tops, desperate to capture his attention. Dominic gave the crowd one devastatingly handsome grin, then focused wholly and completely on the game.

Melissa fell irrevocably in love.

Her adolescent hormones rose up, begging to be released. She'd never reacted like this to anyone: not the cutest boy in school, not the latest pop star. She'd never felt so much admiration for the way a football player handled the ball, with confidence but no unnecessary flash. She'd never gotten tingly all over just because a guy's black hair curled at the base of his neck.

The day Dominic signed on with her father's agency was her best—and worst—day rolled into one. Seeing him on a regular basis at agency events helped her gather lots of erotic data for her ever-growing fantasies about him. If only she didn't always make such a fool of herself around him! Her brain sputtered helplessly; her mouth said stupid things; she walked into tables and spilled drinks.

That Christmas, Dominic DiMarco was laughing with her father in front of the fire, a big-breasted blonde on his arm. The beautiful girl was tall and thin and perfectly dressed—everything Melissa expected one of Dominic's girlfriends to be.

Melissa cringed as she caught sight of her reflection in a serving tray on the kitchen counter. She had a drawer full of expensive makeup she'd never had the guts to use . . . until today. Instead of pulling her unruly curls into a tight ponytail, she'd brushed her hair until it formed a halo around her head like a lion's mane. She wasn't sure if her new hairstyle was better than the ponytail, but at least it was more grown-up. As for clothes, since she attended a private school that required a uniform, she didn't have much to choose from. She'd finally decided on a pair of snug black pants her mother had bought her last year and a tight red sweater she'd borrowed from her much skinnier best friend Alice.

Watching the beautiful men and women chat, Melissa's hands grew damp and her stomach started to hurt. There was no way she could go out there; she could never compete with the supermodels enjoying her family's hospitality.

She turned to leave just as her father caught sight of her. "Melissa, come out and say hello to everyone."

Licking her suddenly dry lips nervously, praying she wouldn't make a fool of herself in front of Dominic, Melissa slowly pushed through the kitchen door and walked into the living room.

"What's that on your face?" her father exclaimed in a loud, slightly drunk voice. "And what the hell are you wearing?"

Twenty pairs of eyes turned her way, the Christmas CD playing in the background actually began to skip, and all conversation stopped.

Dying of embarrassment, Melissa barely noticed her mother moving to her side in support. Her father's blunt remarks had often hurt her feelings, but never this badly. She wanted to run out of the room, but her feet felt as heavy as bags of cement.

Desperately hoping no one else had heard her father's comments, she forced a smile. "Hi, guys," she said with a dumb little wave. She avoided Dominic's gaze. "Merry Christmas."

Two dozen gorgeous, talented men and women smiled back at her with varying degrees of pity in their eyes. It was the most awful, embarrassing moment of her life.

Her father turned to open a bottle of Cristal, and she was about to make a break for her bedroom when he peered at her again. "And what on earth did you do to your hair? It looks like you have a big orange basketball on your head."

Tears sprang to Melissa's eyes just as Dominic said, "Stop upsetting the kid." He turned to face her. "You look great," he lied, then gestured to the table of appetizers. "Are you hungry?"

Dominic's girlfriend coughed behind her hand, but Melissa knew she was disguising a giggle. Feeling like a freak show, Melissa shook her head. "I should get back to my homework now."

As soon as she turned away, her tears started falling. Dominic DiMarco would never look at her as anything other than a stupid little girl. Never.

*

Melissa looked up from her vivid memory to find everyone looking at her and felt her cheeks flush. Quickly, she shook off the sense that she was still seventeen, chunky, and painfully insecure. Ten years had passed since then, long enough for Melissa to transform herself from a shy, overweight teenager into a curvy, confident woman. She was currently single by choice, not because she couldn't get a date. No longer in her early twenties, she just wasn't interested in wasting her time dating guys who couldn't possibly be "the one." She was holding out for someone special . . . someone like Dominic.

He stepped out from under the lights and walked to her, and her heart pounded hard and fast.

"Don't worry. I'll be gentle. I promise," he said in a low voice that only she could hear.

She had no idea what he was talking about. But her body reacted to his deep, sexy voice, her nipples beading against her silk bra.

"I think I missed something," she whispered. "Why is everyone staring at me?"

He grinned, his smile slow and full of heat. Melissa felt faint. Did he have any idea of its impact?

He could have any woman as his sex slave with just the white flash of his teeth.

"Benjamin just asked if you'd mind standing in for the female model for a few minutes so he can set his light meter and try out various poses."

Melissa scanned the room. "She was here a minute ago. What happened to her?"

Dominic leaned in close, his breath on her ear sending goose bumps all over her arms. "Her boyfriend just called and broke up with her. It's going to take a while to fix her makeup." He pulled back and stared into her eyes. "I completely understand if you don't want to do it. Someone else could step in instead."

The makeup artist was practically waving her hand in the air at the thought of getting to rub herself like a cat in heat against Dominic under the lights. Melissa couldn't let that happen to him. Besides, she'd have to be crazy not to jump at five minutes of blissful nearness.

She manufactured a wide smile. "No problem. I'd be happy to help."

He took her hand and squeezed it as he led her over to the lights. She'd never thought the day would come when Dominic DiMarco would be holding her hand. His palms were calloused from years of catching footballs, and she couldn't help imagining his hands sliding down her naked body, over her breasts.

Her breath caught at the potent image, then from the incredible real-life sensation of Dominic wrapping a possessive arm around her waist.

"How do you want us to stand, Benjamin?" Dominic asked, the consummate pro after hundreds of photo shoots.

She gave silent thanks that no one expected her to speak. She was too aroused, too amazed that this moment had come to pass. Dominic didn't seem the least bit perturbed about holding her, and she tried not to let his obvious disinterest get her down. Why should he treat her any differently than any other stranger he had to take a photo with?

Benjamin looked through his viewfinder. "Closer. Sexier."

Dominic pulled her closer to him, and she felt the length of his rock-hard quadriceps pressing into her thighs. She'd never been this intimate with a man with such a spectacular body, and it made her a little bit faint. And ridiculously horny.

The photographer grunted, obviously displeased with something. "Melissa, would you mind taking off your sweater? I can't get a handle on anything with all your clothes in the way."

She blinked at him. It was one thing to be held by Dominic with a cashmere barrier between them. It was another entirely to strip down to a silk tank top. Especially when her nipples were this hard.

Sensing her confusion, Dominic whispered, "I think he needs to see how the light bounces off of skin."

Nodding, she reached for the hem of her sweater and pulled it over her head. The photographer's assistant took it from her trembling hands.

The photographer grunted again. "Much better. Now we need to figure a way to make the two of you look like one."

Blood rushed to Melissa's ears and for a moment all she heard was the drumbeat of her pounding heart. How was she going to make it through the next few minutes in one piece?

Following the photographer's suggestions, Dominic pulled her tightly against him, her breasts pressed against the hard wall of his chest, his groin into her lower belly. Butterflies flew madly around in her stomach. Her fantasies of being in his arms hadn't even been close to the reality of him—his heat, his strength, and even his innate gentleness.

"Much better," the photographer said. "Now tilt your head back."

She lifted her chin a couple of inches and Benjamin made a sound of displeasure. "More."

She felt Dominic's steady heartbeat against her chest. "Don't be shy," he said softly. "It's just me. Arch your back and lean into the weight of my arm. I'll hold you steady."

Forcing herself to concentrate on his words, she remembered that he did this sort of thing all the time. They were each just playing a part for an ad shoot. Wrapping her arms around his neck, she allowed herself to relax against him, to relish her role as the woman he desired above all others.

"That's it," the photographer said as he clicked a series of test shots on his digital camera. "Press your lips against her pulse point, Dominic."

Melissa nearly died as his lips made contact with her skin; for a split second she was in heaven.

Then the real model walked back in, and the next thing she knew, Dominic was releasing her and turning his focus to the skinny model, holding her just as close, placing his lips on her skin, while Melissa watched from a stool across the room.

She had been to heaven . . . and now she was in hell.

Ripping her eyes away from Dominic and the gorgeous girl in his arms, she buried herself in her BlackBerry, needing to read every email several times before the words made any sense. Her brain— but mostly her body—kept returning to the memory of Dominic's hard heat against her body, his lips branding her skin. When she finally allowed herself to look up, Dominic had changed back into his own clothes and was sexy as sin in an Outlaws T-shirt and blue jeans. Just thinking about the way he'd held her, how good his lips had felt on her neck, his big hands circling her hips, a flush started working up from her chest to her neck. To mask her instant arousal, she focused her attention on slipping her BlackBerry into its pink leather case . . . and missed by a mile. It smashed onto the cement floor and went skidding under a row of chairs.

Dominic bent down to retrieve it, then removed the pink leather protective case from her fingers and slipped her phone into it.

Sportswriters called Dominic's large, tanned, steady hands "magic." Melissa agreed. Lord knew she'd dreamed about them stroking her skin a thousand times.

"You were great up there, Melissa. A natural."

She couldn't help but beam at his compliment. "I was so nervous."

His dark brown eyes captured hers with an intensity that surprised her. "I couldn't tell. You were perfect."

She swallowed hard. "Thank you."

Her PDA beeped in his hand, and he pulled it back out of the case and handed it to her. It was a text message from Angie, her father's executive assistant. Her father wanted to meet with her at the first available opportunity. Excitement fluttered in her chest.

"Must be a pretty great boyfriend for you to look like that," Dominic said.

Melissa nearly dropped the BlackBerry again. "I don't have a boyfriend." She rushed to dehumiliate herself. "I think my father might be giving me a promotion today." She hadn't planned to confide in Dominic, but she couldn't hold in her excitement.

"That's fantastic," he said and picked up her Louis Vuitton bag. The expensive leather purse looked incredibly small in his big hands. "How about I get you there faster by giving you a ride back to the office?"

He opened the heavy metal warehouse door for her, and she concentrated on walking down the stairs that led to the garage in her impossibly high heels. Knowing she was going to attend Dominic's shoot had meant an extra hour in her closet that morning. By the time she'd left, her bedroom looked like a hurricane had hit it. After trying on a dozen pairs of jeans, dresses, and shoes, she'd finally settled on a simple black dress with a pencil skirt, fishnets, and peep-toe heels, along with the cashmere sweater. Black would blend into the background at the photo shoot, but a little sex appeal never hurt. After what she'd been asked to do with Dominic in front of a room full of strangers, she was glad she'd made an extra effort.

She felt the heat of his body behind her as they made their way down to the underground garage. He opened the passenger door of his sports car for her, then got behind the wheel. She was struck by how much space he took up . . . and the sheer bliss of sharing such an intimate space with the star of her late-night fantasies. At six-foot-three and 230, Dominic wasn't the tallest or biggest Outlaw, but as the star receiver he was the quickest and most agile. Still, he was the most beautiful man she'd ever been near, the most incredible man who'd ever held her close.

"Congratulations on earning your MBA," he said unexpectedly as he pulled into traffic. "I'm not surprised your father has tapped you to be the next agent."

"Thank you," she said, pride in her voice. The late nights of studying, followed by ten-hour days working for her father, had been grueling. She hadn't had a clue that Dominic knew about her degree. The fact that he did was incredibly flattering.

He pulled up in front of the McKnight Agency, one corner of his rugged mouth curving up, and her breath hitched. Fumbling with her seat belt, she picked up her bag and jumped out.

"Melissa?"

Her heart pounding, she leaned down to the open window.

"Good luck," he said. "You're going to be a terrific agent."

*

Dominic sat in his car for several minutes as traffic whizzed by. What the fuck had he been doing flirting with Melissa? She was completely off-limits. Not only was she his agent's daughter, but she deserved so much more than he could ever give her. She deserved a normal guy with a normal life, not a public figure who was carrying around a secret that could blow everything he'd worked for to pieces.

Which hadn't stopped him from watching her all afternoon from across the photographer's studio. Watching and wanting her.

All day long, he'd wanted to touch her. To run his tongue down the crevice between her lush breasts. To feel her nipples pebble against his palms and rub his face against her soft, creamy skin. To lay her down, slide his hands beneath her ass, and stare at her beautiful, naked body. To lick inside her, then swirl his tongue over her clit. To move over her naked body, slide his cock into her heat, and consume her inch by inch. To watch her face as she came, watch her eyes widen in surprise as her climax ripped through her.

For years he'd been haunted by her scent, by the way she licked the corner of her lips when she was concentrating, by the smooth skin on her throat as she swallowed a sip of coffee. He'd wanted her for so long that he could practically taste her; knew she'd be the sweetest thing he'd ever had on his tongue.

And then Benjamin had called her over, and it was all he could do to keep his hard-on at bay in front of the camera. He'd fantasized about touching her for so long that his brain could barely wrap itself around the reality of her soft hips in his hands. Again and again he replayed that moment when she stripped off her sweater—how hard and tight her nipples were, the full, round curves of her breasts. Ecstasy and torture had warred when he pulled her hard against him, harder than he should have, closer than she needed to be. This had been his one chance to touch her, to hold her, and he'd taken as much as he could get. But a sham kiss on her neck didn't even begin to quench his thirst for her.

Now that he'd had a taste of her sweetness, he wanted her more than he ever had.

CHAPTER TWO

Still reeling from her five minutes in Dominic's arms, Melissa locked herself in the ladies' room until she succeeded in wiping all the arousal and excitement from her eyes and face. Then she unlocked the door and headed over to Angie's desk. She'd known her father's executive assistant, a no-nonsense, borderline-scary, type-A woman, practically all her life. And even though she wasn't a little kid anymore, she was still a little afraid of the woman.

"Perfect timing. Tom's ready to have a word with you."

Taking a deep breath, Melissa turned her father's gold-plated doorknob and went in.

Her father didn't look up as she closed the door. "I just spoke with Dominic."

Melissa's heart thumped as she waited to hear what he'd said about her.

"He made it a point to tell me what a pleasure it was working with you today. Said you saved the day."

Masking her delight at the compliment, Melissa said, "He did great at the shoot, as always. Dominic is a real asset to the company."

Her father shrugged. "He was, but he's getting older."

She dropped her bag to the floor and advanced toward her father. "Are you kidding? Dominic is one of the most recognizable faces of football. No speeding tickets, no bar brawls, no hidden babies. He's a playmaker and a moneymaker. Companies are pounding down our door to get him to advertise their products."

Her father clicked on his email, listening with half an ear. "Times have changed. People want to see their favorite stars screw up, then repent. No one's interested in angels anymore."

Melissa's mouth opened, then closed. How could her father speak about him like this? What ever happened to loyalty? What's more, her father was dead wrong about Dominic's appeal.

"Look at Ty Calhoun," her father pointed out. "Fans are even crazier for him now that he screwed his image consultant, then saw the light and married her. Nothing's better than a bad boy turned good."

Melissa had met Ty a few times and found him

to be a very charming lady-killer, but not at all her type. She preferred someone who didn't have anything to prove, who didn't use his sexuality to win over the world, who simply owned it as an integral part of who he was.

But now wasn't the time for her to bite her father's head off. She sat on the chair directly across from him. "What did you want to see me about?"

"Your mother called. Don't forget to bring potato salad to the barbecue this Sunday, or she'll be all over me for not telling you."

Her heart sank. She'd been so certain that he was going to bring up her promotion. Well, since she had his undivided attention, she'd take the direct approach and ask for exactly what she wanted—and make sure she got it.

"Actually, Father, I'm glad you asked to meet with me. I've been wanting to get on your calendar."

He briefly looked up from his computer screen. "Is there a problem?"

"No. My work has been going very smoothly, and I was extremely pleased by the endorsement deal I negotiated for Wilson last Friday." If ever there was a time to toot her own horn, it was now.

"I'll email you some notes on the Martin trade. You can take that over, as well."

She beamed. "Fantastic."

More work and responsibility without "Agent"

on her business card. She was making a differ-
ence in players' lives and she was well paid for an
associate, but she wanted to be recognized for her
achievements rather than for being Tom McKnight's
daughter.

He looked up at her, impatience on his deeply
lined face. "Was there anything else you needed?"

She straightened her spine. "Yes, there is."

He finally took his hands from the keyboard and
sat back in his chair, lacing his fingers across his
stomach.

"I've been working here for five years," she
began. "During that time I've taken on more and
more responsibility, I've earned my MBA, and I've
negotiated several big endorsement deals for key clients."

Her father nodded, and hope bloomed deep in
her chest.

"I deserve to be promoted to agent."

She laid her damp palms on her lap and waited
for her father to speak. As the silence stretched on, a
knot formed in her stomach.

Her father threw his head back and laughed.
"Honey, I thought you already knew this—no one in
this business will ever take a female football agent
seriously. Especially not a cream puff like you."

Melissa shot to her feet as he turned back to his
computer. "What about all the deals I've worked?"

she demanded. "I've done great things for our clients. I've made them—and you—a lot of money."

He waved a hand, dismissing her completely true claims. "They took you seriously because you work for me. Ultimately, everyone knows I'm the one backing the deals. Besides, you aren't tough enough for this business. Agents can't cry when they don't get their way."

He wasn't joking. Not in the least. And Melissa finally realized the truth: Her father had never, ever, not for one second, planned on her becoming an agent. If he had his way, she'd work as an associate for him until the day he retired.

Seeming to notice her dismay, he said, "Don't get me wrong, honey, you've been doing a great job. You're a top-notch associate. All the guys think so."

He was talking to her as if she were a little girl, which, she now understood, was exactly how he viewed her. They all did: his players, the other agents, his secretary.

"Thank you for your time," she said coldly, then walked across the room and closed the door behind her with a soft click. She held her head high as she walked past Angie's desk.

As she quickly navigated the hallway, Melissa's brain spun with plans. She wasn't going to waste a single minute sitting in her cubicle feeling sorry for herself. She wanted to be an agent, and if she couldn't be a McKnight agent, she'd do it someplace else. And she knew exactly where to start.

Barnum's. The secret bar for San Francisco Bay Area professional athletes. It was the only place where the very rich, very sought-after men could shoot some pool without groupies hanging all over them. Rumor had it not one single female fan had crossed the threshold in thirty years.

But she had no doubt she'd get inside. She'd made a whole lot of guys a whole lot of money. They owed her.

Ignoring the forty new emails in her in-box, she picked up her bag and headed for the elevator. On the street, she hailed a cab and gave the driver her best guess at Barnum's address. It was a widely guarded secret, but she'd been privy to enough drunken conversations to pick up a couple of clues to its location.

On a street corner a block from the water in a rather seedy part of town, Melissa paid the driver and stepped into the fading sunlight. She was beginning to wonder if this was such a good idea, just as the sound of laughter drew her attention to a door opening halfway down a dark alley. A rookie defensive lineman stepped out into the daylight.

Bingo! Now all she had to do was figure out a way to get inside.

She strode to the door and pounded on it with

both fists. It was rather cathartic to beat the crap out of a metal door, even if the edges of her hands were starting to throb.

A man opened the door just wide enough for her to see his gold tooth. "Members only."

He closed the door in her face, but rage made her strong. She shoved it open an inch. "These guys know me. Let me in."

He opened the door a foot this time and checked her out from head to toe. He grinned lecherously. "I'm sure they do, babe. Go home. Find a nice boy to marry and make babies with."

She peered over his shoulder into the dark room. Jones Wilson was leaning over the pool table. She'd just made him a bucket of money, more than double the original offer he'd been made to hock tennis shoes. He owed her.

"Jones!" she shrieked over the throbbing rap music.

The bouncer recoiled and covered his ears, giving her the chance to push the door open and lunge past him. She was halfway inside by the time he grabbed her.

"Not so fast," he growled, and she had a feeling she was moments away from being literally tossed out on her ass.

Just in time, Wilson laid down his pool stick. "Melissa McKnight? What are you doing here, girl?"

The bouncer said, "Sorry, man. I told her 'no groupies.' I'll get her out of here."

"She's no groupie, man. She's my agent's kid. Let her go."

"What's up?" Wilson asked when the bouncer headed back behind the bar. "Some problem with the new contract?"

She shook her head. "No, your contract is fine. Let me get a drink and then you can introduce me to your friends."

He frowned. "Seriously? You're staying?"

"You bet I am." He looked shell-shocked, so she decided to give him a few minutes to get used to the idea of her being in the top-secret players' haunt. "Go back to your pool game. I'll let you know when I'm ready for your help."

He looked over his shoulder at the rest of the players in the club, then shook his head. "I don't think this is such a great idea, you being here."

She shrugged and looked around the joint. "Not much of a vibe, but I suppose it grows on you."

Waving him back toward the pool table, she headed over to the empty bar. At least a dozen pairs of eyes were on her. Football, hockey, and baseball players relaxed with beers and video games and pool. There were even a few pro golfers in the mix. She knew their names and teams, but apart from Wilson she didn't know any of them personally. Yet.

There wasn't another bar in the city where she would have felt as at home. She'd grown up around professional athletes, traveled with them, watched games with them, hung out with their families. Football meant family to her.

"Gin and tonic, please," she said to the beefy bouncer/bartender. "Make it a double."

Looking none too happy about serving her, he grabbed a tall glass.

She took a sip, which immediately turned into a gulp. "God, this is good," she murmured.

Even better than the drink was the instant buzz that worked its way from her head to her toes. She hadn't eaten since 6 a.m. It wasn't going to take long for the drink to work its magic.

"Honestly," she said to the large bartender, "I understand why you wouldn't let me come inside."

"You do, huh?"

She nodded. "These guys need somewhere to get away from everything. The press, the groupies, the big-money pressure. I think it's great that you turned this joint into a refuge." She crossed her fingers over her heart. "I'll never tell. Cross my heart and hope to die."

They'd gotten off to a rocky start, but another drink later proved that the bartender—his name was Ellis—was a very nice man. He was happy to listen to her plans to become the next great football agent.

The next thing she knew, her second drink was empty and he was sliding another one across the bar.

When Ellis flipped the channel to ESPN, they were doing a profile on the greatest wide receivers of all time. Dominic was their top pick, and something warm and heady bloomed in Melissa's chest. She'd chat up the players in the bar later. For the next hour, she was going to nurse her drink along with her pointless crush on the most beautiful man in the world.

CHAPTER THREE

Dominic sprinted the last hundred yards on the track, beating Ty Calhoun by an inch. They fell down on the grass inside the track and sucked in air. "I never thought I'd see the day when an old man like you would beat me," Ty said, panting.

Dominic laughed through the stitch in his side and the throbbing in his knee. "Marriage has made you slow," he ribbed, even though they both knew it was his job as wide receiver to be the fastest guy on the field.

"What can I say? I've got better things on my mind than a leather ball." Ty grinned. "Nothing beats an insatiable new wife waiting at home."

Dominic was happy for his friend, who was one of the best quarterbacks in the country. Things had been iffy there for a while. Fortunately, everything had ended up working out for Ty. Playboy no more, he was a happily married man.

"What about you?" Ty asked as he started a set of sit-ups. "Got marriage and kids in your future any-time soon?"

An image of Melissa popped into Dominic's head, all luscious curves and plump red lips and an almost accidental sensuality. Blood rushed to his groin.

His agent's daughter was as off-limits as they came. Even if she had looked better than ever this morning at the ad shoot, even if her lush curves had been a perfect fit in his hands, even if she had the softest skin he'd ever touched. He wondered for the thousandth time what she'd look like without her clothes on; if the skin on her breasts, her stomach—between her legs—would be as creamy and tempt-ing as her beautiful face.

Shit. He needed to force the picture of Melissa naked and flushed in his bed from his brain. He rolled over and propped himself on his palms for a punishing set of push-ups. "The last girl I dated kept confusing baseball with football."

"Hey, I think I dated her, too," Ty said, laughing. "At least she was hot, right?"

Dominic held his final push-up an inch from the grass for twenty seconds to push himself to the limit. Letting his weight down slowly, he said, "I guess."

The girl had been too skinny and synthetic-looking, with the same overplumped lips and siliconed breasts and skinny ass as every other good-looking blonde that guys like him dated.

The sun was starting to set as they headed into the showers. Dominic stood under the hot spray for several minutes. An integral part of his job with the Outlaws was turning on the charm. Not just on the field, but at charity events and after-hours parties for the media. But he'd always kept a firm check on himself around Tom McKnight's daughter—regardless of the fact that he wanted to fuck her senseless. She might have been the best-looking woman for miles, but she was meant for some other lucky bastard. Not only would Tom never forgive him for touching his little girl, but Dominic was too old for her, too experienced.

He'd grappled with the darkness within himself one too many times, and come up on the losing end. She deserved better than him.

He stepped off the slick tile to dry off, then pulled on his jeans and a T-shirt. He didn't spend much time in bars anymore, having burned through that kind of behavior in high school, but tonight he felt like having a beer. Someplace out of the public eye where he could hang with the guys, shoot some pool, and stop thinking about the beautiful woman that he couldn't have.

The sun was sinking halfway into the Bay as he drove along the Embarcadero toward Barnum's.

Every once in a while, a guy needed a place to get away from the fans. Heck, some of the guys went to get away from their wives and girlfriends.

To the rest of the world, professional athletics looked like a big party. In truth, millions were on the line with every play, every tackle. Sunday's game kicked the shit out of you and your body hurt like hell, with recovery taking the whole week. After spending Monday through Friday in ice baths and murderous massages after practice, you were lucky if you woke up Saturday morning feeling halfway normal, only to head into another grueling Sunday game.

But even though he hurt more lately than he ever had—his shoulder was throbbing from his workout and his knee kept popping—Dominic didn't have any complaints. He wasn't sitting behind a desk. He wasn't putting on a roof in 110-degree weather. He just wasn't healing as fast as he used to.

Dominic parked his car in Barnum's dark, cramped garage, then stepped into the dirty alley and punched in the security code next to the black metal fire door. The lock clicked open and he stepped inside, giving his eyes a moment to adjust to the dim lighting.

Several of the usual suspects were there—a handful of local hockey and baseball players, in addition to several Outlaws. And then his eyes landed on an unexpected sight: A woman with wavy hair was sitting on a bar stool. Her back was to him and her feet were bare, her shoes haphazardly discarded on the floor beneath her seat.

Even as he wondered what in the hell a woman was doing inside Barnum's, his cock instantly reacted to her lush ass, her tight waist, and the ample breasts hinted at from behind the curve of her elbow. A voice in his head told him this woman could be the perfect substitute for Melissa—at least for the night.

The other players were watching her, too, mountain lions silently hunting their prey, ready to sink their teeth into her neck at the first sign of weakness. Protective urges warred with arousal within Dominic, and he accepted his inevitable decision. It was his duty to get her out of there before something bad happened.

These were mostly good guys, but every now and again a bad seed slipped in, particularly among the rookies, who no one really had a good handle on for a couple of years. They were too fresh, too excited about their new pro status. Sometimes they did stupid things—picked up the wrong kind of girl, turned a video camera on, or posted something indecent on the Internet, especially when they were drunk.

Dominic knew firsthand about fucking up, about how a string of stupid decisions could come to a head in a single moment and almost ruin everything.

His face grim, he headed for the woman. She was

talking with Ellis, laughing about something playing on the TV. A warning bell went off in his head, the same kind that he heard on the field just before he got crushed by a defender when coming down with the ball.

Her laugh was husky. Sensual.

And oddly familiar.

Oh, shit.

Melissa McKnight, the woman he wanted to chain to his bed and not let loose until he'd fulfilled every last one of his sexual fantasies, had infiltrated Barnum's.

Anger rode him as he crossed the barroom. She'd been in this business long enough to know that any girl who got drunk around a pro would be easy prey. Sitting there looking as incredibly hot as she did was simply asking for it. She might as well get up on one of the pool tables, strip off all her clothes, and beg one of these guys to take her any damn way he wanted to.

He was nearly at her side when she turned and saw him. "Dominic!" she cried, his name blurring around the edges. "I was just watching you on TV." She blinked up at him like he was her birthday and Christmas presents rolled into one.

He followed her loose-limbed gesture to the large screen hanging above the bottles. ESPN was showing a clip of him making an over-the-shoulder touchdown reception.

"You're so amazing," she murmured, leaning toward him. "So fast. So big."

Her innocent compliments gave him a sudden, raging hard-on. Trying to ignore his body's instinctive response to her nearness, he wrapped his fingers around her upper arm.

Her skin was too warm. Too soft. Too inviting.

His fury at the way she was putting herself in danger merged with his frustration over losing the battle with his dick. "What the hell are you doing here?"

Her tongue flicked out to the corner of her mouth. Sweet lord, he had to look away from her mouth. That way lay madness.

"It's a secret," she whispered.

She tilted her head back to giggle, and his eyes got stuck on the rapidly beating pulse in her long, smooth neck. Her skin was rose-tipped perfection, her hair a mix of blond and brown and auburn that made him want to run his fingers through it for hours just to determine which color it really was.

"I'm taking you home," he said, his voice gruffer than he'd intended. "Now."

Melissa didn't budge. "No, thanks." She picked up her glass and drank the last drop, her tongue snaking out to lick it up.

Dominic's dick twitched as she ignored his command. He'd always assumed that she was soft, pliant. Her easy refusal of his wishes actually made his dick harder. He forced images of her tying him up and straddling him out of his head. A wiser woman would have known not to mess with him. But she'd obviously spent too many years surrounded by big, burly football players who treated her like a little sister. She thought she was safe from him.

She wasn't.

CHAPTER FOUR

Waggling her fingers at Ellis, Melissa lifted her empty glass. With her other hand, she patted the busted-up leather bar stool next to hers. "Sit down, Dominic. Keep me company."

Her long lashes covered her guileless eyes as she stared at his crotch. Shit, she wasn't actually assessing his package, was she? His cock grew another painful inch beneath his jeans. If his fans could see just how badly the "master of control" was losing control, they'd boo him off the field.

"We can do this the easy way," he said in a low voice, "or we can do it the hard way."

She spun slightly to face him, her full mouth curving up slightly. A mouth like hers should be illegal. He had a distinctly uncomfortable memory of her coming home from college five years ago transformed into a goddess with sinfully plump red lips and curves that could make a man crazy.

Curves that *did* make him crazy.

Lifting her gaze from his crotch, she murmured, "Tell me more about doing it the hard way."

Focused on how badly he wanted to taste her lips, it took him several seconds to realize that she'd infused the word *hard* with a sexual undertone. Quickly, he reminded himself that it was because she was drunk.

Melissa always maintained an impressive professionalism around the guys. The way she was acting had nothing to do with him. After lord knew how many drinks, she would have probably come on to any guy in any bar. Which was all the more reason why he had to get her out of there.

In a flash, he had her up off the bar stool and hoisted over his shoulder, her sweet ass in his hands, her breasts pressing into his shoulder blades. He expected her to scream, to insist that he put her down. Instead, she shifted her hips more firmly into the curve of his palm.

"Mmmm, you're strong," she murmured as he strode across the cement floor.

Several of the guys whistled, and some had the nerve to clap. "You go, Dom," one called, and Dominic scowled fiercely at them, making a mental note to kick each and every one of their asses for thinking dirty thoughts about Melissa.

Wilson smiled at him. "Thanks for taking her

out of my hair. Watching over her ass was too much responsibility for me."

In less than sixty, they were out of the bar and he'd strapped her into his passenger seat. He tried to keep contact to a minimum as he leaned across her body to click her seat belt into place, but he couldn't avoid pressing his triceps into her breasts. By the time he got behind the wheel, warning himself for the hundredth time to cool off, she was curled up in the leather seat, looking like a cat nestled in a comfortable blanket. Her eyes were warm honey as they raked over him. He'd never seen her like this, with her guard down.

She was all woman . . . and on the prowl for a man.

Deciding that his wisest bet was to play the role of concerned friend, he said, "I'm taking you back to my place for coffee. You're going to sober up, and then you're going to tell me how the hell you ended up in Barnum's."

Something must have happened between the photo shoot and Barnum's—probably something at work. As soon as she filled him in on the details, he would fix the problem.

He wasn't a fool, though. Women hated men who tried to solve their problems, so he just wouldn't let her know about it.

In a warm voice Melissa said, "I've always wanted to see your house."

She wrapped her forearms around her shins. He'd forgotten to grab her shoes on the way out, and his erection grew yet again at the sight of her red toenails peeking out from beneath her very sexy fishnets.

He cleared his throat, working to obliterate all signs of lust from his tone. "I'm taking you now."

She all but purred, "Goodie. I've been waiting a long, long time for you to take me."

Jesus, if she only knew all the ways he wanted to take her, she'd throw herself out of his car. She was innocent and pure, and had no idea about the dark side of life—or men.

He turned into his building's parking garage a couple of minutes later. Melissa was silent; maybe she'd fallen asleep, he thought. Sick bastard that he was, he wouldn't mind having an excuse to pick her up and carry her upstairs. She could have his bed. Potent images filled his brain: of her naked between his sheets, standing beneath the spray of water in his shower, drying between her legs with a towel.

Working to shake off the X-rated images, he looked over, surprised to see her staring right at him, her amber eyes wicked and wanting.

It was pretty obvious that she'd had a crush on him in her teens, but she'd never looked at him like this before—like she wanted to unzip his pants and throat his cock right then and there.

Fuck.

"Stay there," he cautioned as he came around to her side. The last thing he needed was for her to fall out of his car and smack her head on the cement floor. He opened the passenger door and held out his hands. Once they got upstairs, he was going to make her a pot of coffee, then sit on the opposite side of his living room while she drank it.

She wobbled a bit and he instinctively pulled her into his chest to steady her. Her breasts were criminal, the way their full weight settled against him.

"You know what?" she whispered as she slid an arm around him, gliding her fingertips over his triceps and lats. "I think I like doing things the hard way."

She lowered her face to his shoulder and her hair tickled his chin. It was killing him to keep his hands off her.

Purposefully ignoring the seductive intent of her words, he said, "You'll feel much better once you've had some coffee."

Her smile was lazy as he propelled her into the elevator. She relaxed into his body, and he was amazed, despite himself, at how well they fit together, her soft heat the perfect foil for his solid mass.

"I already feel better," she said with a soft smile.

If he hadn't been so attuned to her every heartbeat, to the way her nipples had peaked beneath her black dress, he might have missed it when she added, "Now that you're here," in a near whisper.

His cock grew another inch beneath the zipper of his jeans. She wasn't making this easy for him. He unlocked his front door and led her into his foyer. Dropping his keys on the front table, he guided her into his large kitchen. Both his kitchen and living room were fronted with floor-to-ceiling glass. Lights from cars, boats, and houses across the Bay gleamed into the granite-and-cherrywood–clad room. True to his Italian roots, Dominic prided himself on being a great cook. Not that Melissa was ever going to find out. If he could barely control himself over coffee, he sure as hell wouldn't be able to keep his dick in his pants through an entire meal.

Melissa moved out of his arms and headed straight to the windows. He put on a very strong pot of coffee, and when he turned back to her he nearly laughed out loud. She'd pressed herself up against the window, her palms flat against the glass. The laughter died in his throat as he imagined coming up behind her, yanking up her skirt, sliding down her stockings, and sinking into her wet heat. Her full breasts would be heavy in his hands, her nipples hard between his fingertips.

His famously steady hands were shaking as he brought over a large mug of coffee. Hearing his approach, she turned and said, "What a beautiful view."

She was far more beautiful than any view, and he couldn't take his eyes off her—couldn't stop the increasingly pornographic images of the two of them naked and sweaty from running through his head.

"Yeah," he finally replied, "it's nice." He took her hand and guided her to the plush couch. "Drink."

God, he sounded like a caveman. He'd never been nervous in front of cameras or out in a stadium playing in front of one hundred thousand screaming fans. So how could one curvy woman make it so hard for him to string more than two words together?

She tucked her legs beneath her and picked up the mug. Bringing the rim up to her lips, she took a sip, staring unabashedly at him over the mug.

"I really do like your place," she said, "but something's missing."

You're missing.

The words jumped uncensored into his brain. Because even with the views and the nice furniture and the gourmet kitchen, she was right: His house had never quite felt like home. Until now, with Melissa curled up on his couch, eating him up with her eyes.

Bringing her here had been a bad plan. A very bad plan.

Because he didn't need to save her from the other players in Barnum's. He needed to save her from himself.

CHAPTER FIVE

Dominic had been her very own warrior, swooping in from the darkness to carry her on his shoulder away from all those big bad athletes. That, and being held captive in his car and his condominium, was the most exciting thing that had ever happened to her. He'd picked her up as if she hardly weighed a thing and she'd felt tiny and perfect.

Plus, she thought with a small smile, she was nearly certain she'd felt his raging hard-on in the elevator. Which meant he wanted her.

The gin and tonics were starting to wear off, and she missed the warm, blurry cocoon that had helped her flirt so easily in the bar. She put down the coffee mug and stood up, stretching slowly, making sure that Dominic could see every curve.

"I'm not quite ready for coffee," she said as she went into the kitchen. She looked around for a wine rack, pulled out a bottle of merlot, and held it up. "Care for a glass?"

He shot to his feet. "No. And I don't think you should have any more, either."

She shrugged. "One it is." Opening and closing his cupboards until she found the red-wine glasses, she poured herself a generous amount. She lifted the glass to her nose and inhaled. "Mmm. This smells lovely."

She glanced up to see how Dominic was reacting, and was disappointed to see him sitting on a bench carved from a tree trunk on the opposite side of the room. Well, that wouldn't do at all.

He leaned forward, his elbows on his knees. "Tell me what happened today."

She carried her glass to the couch nearest to him. "Nothing out of the ordinary." Which was true. Now that she realized her father had never respected her, the things he'd said to her today weren't much of a surprise.

Dominic's stare didn't waver. "A girl like you doesn't get drunk at a bar for no reason."

"Why don't you tell me, then," she asked in a husky voice. "Why *does* a girl like me get drunk at a bar?"

He stiffened and she hid a smile. She hoped he was stiff all over.

Rather than answer her provocative question, he stood up, retrieved her coffee mug, and put it on the side table next to her. He reached for her wineglass. "I'll take that."

He was incredibly sexy when he got all caveman on her, but she had no intention of handing over her glass. She was a big girl who knew when enough was enough. And she definitely hadn't had enough tonight, especially since both of them were still fully clothed.

Seduce him.

She closed her eyes. It sounded good. So good. What she wouldn't give for one night with him, for the chance to finally live out all her fantasies.

Seduce him.

How could she resist? He was everything she'd ever wanted, and there was no denying his attraction to her—not when his erection was so clearly outlined by his jeans. Her skin felt sensitive as she stood up and moved directly in front of Dominic. He couldn't back up without conceding defeat, and she relished being so close to the heat of his body, to all those delicious muscles. Waves of heat pulsated between her legs and delicious shivers worked their way up her spine.

She held the wineglass between her breasts. "Come and get it."

✳

A sharp pain split Dominic's temple. If it had been anyone else, he would have sworn that she was trying to seduce him. But Melissa? No way.

Her words had to be innocent, but his mind kept

turning them around until he couldn't keep things straight anymore. Lord, if she only knew exactly *what* he wanted to come and get.

Her breasts were rapidly rising and falling, and the red wine nearly sloshed over the glass and onto her soft skin. Just thinking about it made him nearly blow right there in his pants. Hell, he could reach out and rip her dress off in seconds. And then she'd be naked and his for the taking.

He was losing the battle between right and wrong. They were blurring together, tempting him to find out if her thighs were as soft as they looked. He was this close to pulling her against him, to getting his hands on her. All over her.

He clenched his jaw and reached for the glass. But she was standing so close that his wrist rubbed up against her breasts, and her nipple beaded against him. He wrapped his fingers around hers on the stem of the glass, but he was so hard he couldn't control a damn thing anymore. Wine splashed out of the glass, rolling down into her cleavage. God, how he wanted to lick it from her skin in long strokes.

"This is my favorite dress," she whispered. "I need to get the stain out before it sets."

Then she stripped off her dress and stood in his living room wearing the sexiest black-and-red lingerie he'd ever seen.

Dominic couldn't take his eyes off her. He'd never

been so attracted to a woman, never seen anyone so beautiful. His fingers itched to stroke her skin, to undo the clasp at her back, to slide her panties down her thighs and watch them fall to the rug.

"I'm sorry," he said, trying to speak over the gravel in his throat. "I should stop staring."

She looked up at him, her eyes full of desire. "Please," she said, and arousal hit him like a sledge-hammer. "Don't stop."

All his blood rushed to his cock. "You don't mean that."

She moved closer. "I do. I want you to touch me. To kiss me." She dropped her voice to a whisper. "I want you to make love to me, Dominic."

In seconds, his hands were in her hair, his mouth on hers. He knew that his kiss was rough, that he should stop his palms from moving down her shoulders, over her breasts, that he shouldn't be shoving his hard, denim-clad thigh between her naked legs. But he couldn't stop. Nothing had a chance of getting between him and her sweet pussy anymore.

He felt her surprise as he pounced on her, but they were long past the time when she could have retreated. She'd said she wanted him to fuck her, and now she was going to get her wish.

He was going to fuck her long and hard, and he wasn't going to let her go until he finally got her out of his system.

She gasped as he lifted her up onto his hips. His shoulder injury throbbed but he ignored the ache.

Kneading her soft flesh with his hands, teasing her lips with his mouth, he backed her up against the window, pressing her into it. He ran kisses along her jaw to the hollow of her neck, and she arched her neck to give him better access. Her breasts rose and his lips were greedy, desperate for a taste of her nipples. He sucked one hard, rosy tip into his mouth and she moaned in pleasure.

Wanting his hands free, he propped her up against the glass wall with the weight of his body. "Hold on tight, sweetheart."

She wrapped her wrists around his neck and locked her ankles together behind his waist. She was so damn hot, her heat cupping his cock even through the thick denim of his jeans.

He cupped her breasts in his hands, pushing them together, tonguing her nipples. He could spend all night loving them, nibbling on her soft flesh, listening to her whimper. Next time, he would give her breasts the attention they deserved. Right now he couldn't help but slide his fingers down between her labia.

He found slick, slippery flesh.

She gasped, "Dominic," as she pushed closer to his fingers.

He covered her mouth with his and found her

tongue in the exact moment he plunged one finger into her tight, wet pussy. She bucked against him and he slid his other fingers over her lips.

"Sweet lord, you're wet," he murmured as he toyed with the tight bud of her clitoris, getting lost there for several moments.

She ground her hips against his hand. "Please, Dominic," she begged, "Please."

He knew what she was asking for. She wanted to come, with his fingers on her. And he would let her, this first time. Next time, it would be his mouth. And then his cock, deep inside her.

Increasing the pressure on her clit, swirling tight, hard circles that made her breath come in fast gasps, he let go of her ass and slid his other hand down toward her cunt, too. He wanted to feel her ride his fingers, feel her climax throbbing against his knuckles.

Needing to see her face, her eyes, he pulled away from her mouth, let off on her clit just slightly, and slid another finger into her pussy.

Her eyes flew open, her irises dilated with passion. Sweet lord, she was going to be a tight sheath.

"Come for me, sweetheart."

She grasped the back of his neck with her hands and pulled his mouth onto hers as her muscles clamped down tight on his fingers. Her tongue invaded his mouth as she pumped up and down on his hand. He'd had never wanted a woman this much, had never been so desperate to spread her pussy lips wide and fuck her.

Her hips slowed as her climax subsided, and even though he was still harder than he'd ever been before, he softened their kiss.

He slid his fingers out and shifted his body away from hers, knowing that her legs must be tired from clasping them so tightly around his waist. Now he wanted to take her to his bed and explore every last inch of her perfect skin with his mouth and hands.

CHAPTER SIX

The V between her legs was buzzing with sensation as Dominic picked her up and carried her down the hall. He had the most powerful, marvelous hands. Strong, yet gentle enough to tease her until she was desperate for release. And his fingers were so long, so skilled. No wonder he was one of the top wide receivers in the NFL, his hands were definitely magic.

Every Sunday, Dominic was the most focused man on the field. And when he was touching her, it was as if no one else on earth existed. She'd never been with a man who was so wholly focused on giving her pleasure.

She shivered, thinking about what he'd done to her. And what she hoped he was going to do next.

"Looks like you need me to warm you up," he said, and she continued trembling in excited anticipation.

They were just at the threshold of his bedroom, when he bent his dark head down to her breasts. She felt his warm breath on her nipple and then he covered the stiff peak with his mouth, his tongue swirling and teasing, and then his lips sucking and pulling at it.

Instinctively, she arched into his mouth. She'd never been loved like this, by a man who possessed a map of the most responsive parts of her body.

"I can't get enough of your breasts," he growled.

If she'd had one final coherent thought left in her brain, she would have come back with something sexy. But then he was laying her down on the soft covers of his bed and she was enveloped in softness on one side, and heat and hard muscles on the other. No woman could have used her brain at a time like this.

Dominic kneeled over her, and she reached for the hem of his T-shirt.

"I want you naked, too," she urged as she explored the deep indentations of his abdominal muscles with her fingertips. His stomach twitched beneath her touch and Melissa suddenly became aware of her womanly strength.

Dominic had controlled her heart and body for so many years, she wanted *him* to know what it was like. At least for one night.

She put her hands on the button of his jeans, but he gently covered her fingers with his own.

"Not yet."

As frustration bubbled inside her, he said, "I can't wait another second to taste you again." Then he began kissing his way down her naked body—from her cheek to her shoulders, along the sides of her breasts, her rib cage, all the way past her belly button. She was holding her breath, waiting for the blissful moment when he would touch her with his tongue, but instead he gently nipped at the inside of her thigh, the back of her knee, her ankles, her big toe.

Trembling inside and out, she realized she was going to come again without Dominic so much as touching her clit. Desperate for release, her vaginal muscles clenched convulsively as Dominic's kisses traveled back up her calves, up her thighs. At last she felt his hands on her hips, opening her up to him.

"Wait for me, sweetheart," he said, and she expected his tongue and lips to make contact with her heated flesh. Instead, he blew a long breath across her clitoris.

She cried out in surprised ecstasy.

His hands cupped her butt cheeks and he lifted her closer to his mouth and blew again. Air rushed across her mound and she whimpered again with pleasure.

"You like it when I blow on you, don't you?" he said, his words teasing her to an even higher fever pitch.

"Again," she begged, desperate for release. "Do it again."

She held her breath until the sweet moment when another firm breath lashed across her clit. Then she couldn't stop herself from reaching for his head, from pushing herself against his mouth.

All she wanted was to come with his tongue on her.

In her.

As if he could hear her silent plea, he slid his tongue from one edge of her labia to the other, pushing hard against her intensely aroused flesh. Her second climax hit her without warning, and she spiraled higher and higher as he entered her with his tongue, pushing deep, driving her all the way over the edge.

Everything was spinning around and around, and it had nothing to do with the gin and tonics. Being with Dominic was so incredible, so mind-blowing, that she could barely take it in.

When she opened her eyes. Dominic's face was dark and gorgeous above hers. He was levered on his arms above her and smiling a wicked, sultry smile that did crazy things to her insides. She'd already come twice beneath his magical fingers and mouth, and she wanted more of him. *All* of him.

"Okay," he said, "how about you take my clothes off now?"

Her answering smile was equally wicked. Now that the edge had been taken off, she wanted to tease him the way he'd teased her. To make him feel as good as he'd made her feel.

She moved her hands beneath his shirt and all clear thinking fled. He was hard and rippled and felt so damn good to touch. She pulled his shirt up over his head. "I want you naked and in me. Now."

"Thank God," he said as he reached for a condom from his bedside drawer. "I need to be inside you, too. Believe me. I'm dying for it."

Her fingers shook as she fumbled with the button on his jeans, and he gently helped her unzip him. His cock sprang free, pushing into her belly. He slid off his jeans and boxers, then handed her the condom.

She'd never seen anything as glorious as Dominic's thick, hard cock. He was so big. And more than one lover had commented on how "tight" she was.

Sensing her apprehension, he guided her hands over the head of his shaft, helping her unravel the rubber sheath. "You were made for me, *cara bella.*"

His tender words were a sensual caress. Shifting beneath his heavy weight, she opened her legs wide. He settled between her thighs, the tip of his dick teasing her clit.

Holding the bulk of his weight off her, he bent his head and took her lips in a sweet, gentle kiss. As he slowly loved her mouth, his tongue tasting every corner, every crevice, he slid his thick, hard shaft into her, unhurriedly stretching her, giving her more of him than she'd thought humanly possible.

He pulled back from her mouth and whispered against her skin, her neck, her hair, "You're so wet. So hot. So tight." He pushed in another inch and she shifted her hips to take him even deeper. "So damn tight."

She'd never felt so good, like her body was being molded and shaped by him. He was so careful, so patient, and she could feel his restraint in the tautness of his back muscles, the faint sheen of sweat on his skin.

She wanted to take whatever he offered. She craved all of him, every ounce of his passion and desire. He seemed to read her mind, for he shifted them so that he was lying on the bed and she was on top, straddling his cock.

His hands moved over her breasts and he rolled her nipples between his thumbs and forefingers as he slid in and out of her with slight hip rolls.

Instinctively, she settled down another inch on his shaft. He sucked in a breath, then put just enough pressure on her lower back with his hands to bring her breasts perfectly in line with his mouth. He cupped them together and she nearly came again when his teeth grazed her sensitive nipples, his cock only halfway inside.

She couldn't take it anymore. Sliding down on

his erection, she took the rest of him, and before she knew it, he'd rolled them over again and was bucking into her, unleashing all the power he'd been holding back. She held on to his back and shoulders, sinking her teeth into the cords on his neck as he drove into her so hard and deep that she wanted to scream with pleasure.

He found her mouth again and kissed her like she'd never been kissed before, like he was trying to possess her soul. His pelvic bone ground against her clit and his cock plunged inside her and she couldn't think, could barely breathe. The only thing she could do was head into the most explosive climax of her life.

He continued to thrust into her, slower now, and she couldn't wait another second for him to join her. Her muscles clenched tightly around him a moment before he groaned her name, and she felt him contract and explode inside her tight canal.

They clung to each other as the spasms heightened, then slowly retracted. Melissa had never felt so good—or so exhausted.

This had been her worst day . . . and then her very, very best.

*

Dominic heard her soft, even breathing and knew she was asleep. Everything had spun out of control so quickly. But now that Melissa lay naked and warm in the crook of his arm, now that he could focus on something other than his raging hard-on, it was time to take a hard look at what he'd done.

His brain told him to get out of bed and wait in the living room until she woke up, but his body refused to listen. Even though he'd just committed the cardinal sin of mixing business with pleasure.

The bitter taste of remorse was hard to swallow. Dominic had always prided himself on not screwing his way through the crowds of women who surrounded the Outlaws. He'd always been discriminating, always made his intentions clear. He had a powerful sex drive and he loved everything about being with a woman, but he'd never said "I love you." He wasn't sure that he even had it in him. He'd watched his mother screw up relationships with too many men to believe that love was something the DiMarcos knew how to do. Which was why he didn't give women false expectations.

Screwing Melissa was the biggest mistake he'd ever made.

But even as he despised himself for taking her so ruthlessly, all he wanted was to run his hands over her lush ass, slide his fingers into her slick heat, and hear her cry out his name again. His dick twitched against her thigh, and he couldn't stop himself from cupping one full, perfect breast. Her nipple beaded in his palm and he accepted that there was no turning back, no sending her home tonight.

Tomorrow he'd deal with the consequences and repent.

She shifted drowsily against him and her eyes fluttered open. Surprise registered in her sleepy eyes.

"Dominic, am I really in your bed?"

He murmured, "Yes," against her lips, then gently shifted her weight so that her ass was pressed against his erection. She rocked against him and he reached for another condom. "I need to be inside you again."

"What are you waiting for?" she asked, her voice soft and warm.

His cock grew another inch at her invitation. He played with the fullness of her breasts, the hardness of her nipples as he sheathed himself with the condom, then opened her thighs with his knee.

She had to be sore from the way he'd spread open her incredibly tight pussy just a short time ago, but he had to have her—had to feel the sweet pressure of her climax squeezing him, giving him the most intense pleasure he'd ever known.

He found the entrance to her slick pussy and slid inside her in one fast thrust. Her breath whooshed out in a gasp, but all he could think about was how good it felt to be surrounded by her heat.

Slipping one hand beneath her rib cage, he

twisted her nipples with his fingers, allowing his other hand to roam to her slick cunt. Her clit was tight and hard and he rubbed it in time to his thrusts, pushing against her arousal with his fingers as he invaded her with his shaft.

Her breath grew quick and shallow, and knowing that she was on the verge of coming again in his arms, he released the hold on his strict self-control. In moments, her cries of ecstasy mixed with his roars of pleasure. He'd never come so hard or so long, or been squeezed so tight.

Melissa McKnight was the hottest piece of ass he'd ever had. It was going to kill him to walk away from her lush curves and wild sensuality—even if it was the right thing to do.

CHAPTER SEVEN

An unfamiliar whirring sound woke Melissa up. Deep under a plush bedspread and sinfully soft sheets, she opened her eyes. All at once, everything came back to her. Dominic had brought her home from the bar. She'd seduced him and he'd pounced on her and made her every fantasy come to life.

The smell of fresh-ground coffee wafted into the bedroom. Her muscles ached as she stretched. If she had her way, she'd stay naked in Dominic's bed forever.

And he could have his way with her whenever he wanted.

His thrilling words bounced around in her head: *You were made for me.* It was something she'd always known, but she'd never expected him to feel the same way. Happiness flooded through her as she threw back the covers.

She opened the door to his walk-in closet and took a deep breath of his trademark scent—pine trees in summer sun. Taking a white button-down shirt off its hanger, she slipped it on and smiled. She couldn't wait to persuade him to let their coffee grow cold while they went back to bed and explored the daylight hours together.

Although, she thought with a grin, given the way he'd taken her again and again during the night, he wasn't going to need much persuasion.

She brushed her teeth with some toothpaste on one finger and finger combed her hair. Her makeup had worn off during the night, but every time she thought about their intense lovemaking she flushed and her eyes grew bright, so she figured she looked okay without it.

Naked except for his shirt, which hung to her knees, she walked down the hall to the kitchen.

Dominic's back was to her as she stood in the doorway admiring his beautiful physique. His slacks framed his tight butt and his well-pressed, tailored shirt made his shoulders look impossibly broad. Something about his outfit struck her as odd, though. Did he have an appointment this morning? She hoped he'd whip through his meeting and daily summertime workout and be back soon so they could get back to the good stuff.

"Good morning," she said, her voice a bit chirpier than she'd planned. How was it that he still made her nervous, after everything they'd shared?

He slowly turned to face her, and her stomach knotted at his serious expression.

"Melissa." He said her name hard and low, like the pronouncement of a death sentence.

"The coffee smells good," she said, trying to act like nothing was wrong, like there wasn't an enormous white elephant in the room with them. "Where do you keep your mugs?"

He pointed to a cupboard above the dishwasher. She opened the cherrywood door and went on her toes to reach for a mug on the top shelf. His shirt rode up her thighs, showcasing the curves of her bottom, and she desperately hoped he was watching. That he'd remember what he'd done to her just a few hours ago, that he'd remember what he'd said about being meant for each other.

Closing the cupboard door, she turned and held out the mug. His hands were steady as he poured, and she worked to control her nerves as she blew steam off the top.

"I'm sorry," he said into the awkward silence.

His simple words broke her heart. Obviously he regretted the passionate hours they'd shared. And now he had clearly steeled himself to do the right thing, to apologize for making love to her.

She wanted to cry, to scream that it wasn't fair.

She'd thought she was finally going to see her dreams come true; instead, she'd been nothing but a mistake.

A huge mistake, judging by his grim expression.

But the worst thing of all would be if he saw how much his rejection hurt her, so she forced herself to stare back into his dark eyes.

"There is nothing to be sorry about," she said in a surprisingly steady voice.

He looked at her with obvious relief, and she realized that he'd been bracing himself for tears. But she hadn't cried in front of her father, and she wasn't going to cry now.

"You were off-limits," he said, as if that should explain everything. "You still are."

Ten minutes ago she'd foolishly assumed they would start dating, that she'd be his girlfriend, just because he made her come three times in a row. But she'd known all along that it was just one night in heaven, hadn't she? She couldn't get all angry and hurt when he'd never promised her anything else.

"Last night was wonderful," she said honestly. "You're a marvelous lover, Dominic."

Dominic leaned against the black granite counter, only a twitching muscle in his temple betraying his discomfort. "I should never have—"

"I'm glad you did." She didn't want any regrets to spoil the magical night they'd shared. "I'm glad *we* did." She put down her coffee mug. "It's late. I should be heading into the office."

She walked into the living room to get her clothes. She needed to get out of here before she could give in to the hurt.

But Dominic wasn't making it easy on her. He followed her, a big dark presence in the doorway as she dressed.

"I'll make it up to you, Melissa. Just tell me how."

"Stop, please," she said. "We're two adults who wanted to have sex. Let's leave it at that."

But the weight of his remorse hung heavily in the room. "You want to be an agent. I'll be your first client."

His words cut into the armor she'd erected around her heart. He thought he was offering her what she wanted—her first superstar client. Yet she would have given that up a hundred times over if it meant being loved by Dominic every day and every night.

Anger finally burst to the surface. "I don't need any favors. I'm doing fine on my own," she lied.

"Your father won't promote you, will he?"

His question blindsided her. Her fingers stilled on her zipper.

"That's what last night at Barnum's was about," Dominic prodded. "That's why you got drunk. And came home with me." Mild disgust crossed his face.

"I know how your father thinks, how he runs his business. He's honest and he's a hell of a negotiator. But he'll never hire a female agent." He paused. "Not even his own daughter."

Melissa swallowed hard. She hated that he'd already figured everything out. Didn't he see how unfair it was to dangle the ultimate carrot over her head, that even one client of Dominic's stature could set her up to attract other big clients and show her father that he was dead wrong about her being a cream puff?

She shook her head, willing the speeding train in her brain to stop before it crashed into a brick wall. She couldn't accept his offer, couldn't serve her pride up on a plate like that.

"You don't owe me anything," she said again. "We had a night of fun. So what? We've both had one-night stands," she lied.

"You haven't."

She stood her ground. "I have."

"I'll kill him."

She almost smiled at his surprisingly jealous reaction, but she didn't have a smile in her. Not yet.

"You and I had a great night together. No ties, no promises. Stop worrying," she said, putting a hand on his arm to reassure him. But touching him was a big mistake. She rubbed her hand on her hip to stop the tingling. "I'm fine." She would be. One day.

"I'll have my lawyer draw up a contract this afternoon for your review."

She stared at him in disbelief, unable to continue this discussion with him any longer. He was acting like a dictator, yet she was still aroused by him. Every time he moved his arms and his biceps flexed, every time she watched his hands move and thought about what he'd done to her with those long fingers, she started losing the tenuous hold she had over her dignity.

Head held high, she retrieved her bag and walked out the door in her bare feet and down to the elevator. She felt his eyes on her as she pressed the red button and waited for the elevator.

The bell dinged, the stainless steel doors slid open, and she stepped inside. She had to be strong, couldn't let Dominic see how deep his arrows had gone, so she made herself face his stony features as the doors slid closed.

CHAPTER EIGHT

Melissa walked into the office after a long, scalding shower and ages in front of her mirror, working on hair and makeup and clothes. Her brain was at war with her body—her body still in a state of bliss, her mind reeling at being kicked to the curb—but she refused to lie down and play dead.

She wore a snug purple V-neck cashmere sweater she'd stashed at the bottom of a drawer. If ever there was a day for a jolt of confidence, this was it, so she added a wholly unnecessary push-up bra. Paired with perfectly tailored black slacks, she hoped she looked like a million bucks, even if she felt like the ninety-nine-cent special.

For the second day in a row, Angie waylaid her. "Your father has been trying to get a hold of you for hours," she said, her tone both accusing and questioning.

Melissa shrugged. She had more important things

to think about than her father's endless laundry list of tasks. Like getting a new job at a new agency, for instance. Or, even better, starting her own. "You can tell him I'm here now."

She went to her cubicle, sat down at her desk, and logged on to her computer. By the time she left work today, she'd have a list of strong contacts at the top five other agencies in the football business. Scratch that; she wasn't going to limit her search to football. She'd always liked baseball and hockey. Hell, she could learn to like boxing or golf if she had to.

Her phone rang and, foolishly, her first thought was, *Dominic*. But when she looked at the caller ID, it was just Angie calling to say that her father was eagerly awaiting her presence.

Melissa closed her eyes. She *couldn't* get her hopes up every time the phone rang, couldn't waste her life daydreaming that Dominic was going to fall in love with her.

Pushing back her chair, she slipped on a pair of red-rimmed no-prescription glasses she'd bought for the express purpose of looking tougher, more sharply angled. Her father's door was wide open and she sat on his couch, unwilling to subject herself to the seat of torture in front of his desk. Surprisingly, he got up to join her.

He laid a thick file down on the coffee table. "I've given more thought to yesterday's discussion."

He looked intensely uncomfortable, and her first instinct was to say something to put him at ease, to let him think she hadn't been hurt by the way he'd shut down her dreams. But her self-respect rose up and she settled for crossing her legs and waiting for him to continue.

"I've decided to give you full representation of a new client."

Nothing could have shocked her more. "Seriously?"

He rubbed his eyes, suddenly looking his age. "Your mother read me the riot act. Said I wasn't giving you a fair chance."

So Mommy had come to rescue her baby girl, just like she had years ago on the playground, or at the dinner table when her father chastised her for not getting better grades. Which meant that nothing had really changed. Her father didn't really want her to be an agent.

He was simply afraid of his wife.

Melissa stopped her self-pitying thoughts cold. If she wanted to change her life, she needed to focus on the positive. Regardless of her father's reasons for giving her this chance, this was her opportunity to blow his expectations out of the water.

"Who's the player?"

He gestured to the file and she picked it up. JP Jesse. His name vaguely registered on her radar.

"He's been playing for five years. The Tennessee Titans cut him and he was an unrestricted free agent who no one wanted out of the gate in March. In May he was given a tender offer by the Titans, but he's desperate to get out of Tennessee. Which means the clock is ticking on signing him to another team before the free-agent period runs out July twenty-second. And I don't have two weeks to kill finding JP a new contract."

But she did. She flipped through JP's file. He didn't play much, but when he did his stats were impressive, averaging fifteen yards a reception and a touchdown every ten catches.

"Looks like he has potential," she said as she scanned the information.

Her father shrugged. "Maybe. Maybe not."

A warning bell went off in her head. Her father never took on long shots; every last one of his clients was a sure thing. *Oh crap. He's taken on a player to pacify me.*

"Does he drink?" she asked. "Party? Blow it during big games when the pressure's on?"

Her father nodded. "All of the above. The Titans' official reason for releasing him was a DUI he got in January. But after looking through his file, I think he's got bigger problems than partying too hard." He paused. "I'm counting on you to make him into a star wide receiver. Or drop him on his ass."

How the hell was she supposed to do all that in two weeks? Well, this was her chance to prove to her father that she had what it took to be the best damn agent in the business. "Thank you for this opportunity."

Leaving her father's office, she pulled out JP's 8 x 10. A tall, lean, dirty blonde with a wicked gleam in his eyes stared back at her. Unabashed sensuality leaped off the page. They'd start with his looks, then work on his skills. With a face and body like that, if she couldn't get him a new contract, maybe she could negotiate an agreement with a modeling agency.

Engrossed in JP's file, she walked straight into a rock wall. The folder—along with her glasses—went flying as she tried to catch her balance. Strong hands curled around her shoulders and a familiar scent of heat and pine needles assailed her senses.

"Steady now," the wall said as he slid his hands down her arms.

"I'm fine," Melissa muttered into Dominic's chest. "You can let go of me now."

Both bent down to pick up the pages and videos from JP's file. "Thanks," she said, then stood and replaced her glasses. Edging past him in the suddenly small hallway, she dismissed him with a cheerful, "Have a nice day."

But his fingers cupped her elbow. "We need to talk."

Her heart thumped erratically. Couldn't he at least give her twenty-four hours? But this was her father's office, and she had no choice but to listen to his superstar clients.

"Follow me," she said, leading Dominic into the biggest conference room in the agency, one that could hold all forty board members. Unlike the smaller conference rooms, which had glass walls that looked into the main office floor, this one was paneled in glossy mahogany. Now if he would just sit at the far end of the enormous table, she might be able to get through part *deux* of their postscrew chat in one piece.

He pulled out the chair next to hers and her body reacted to his nearness against her will. "What can I help you with?" she asked impersonally.

He handed her a thick sheaf of papers. "Here's our new contract." His eyes were dark and hungry— but still guilty. "I'm yours."

Her nipples peaked and she knew her sweater did nothing to disguise her arousal. How badly she wanted his words to be true. But not like this—not because he thought he owed her for having sex with her.

Shaking her head, she slid the papers back to him. "I've already got my first client," she said, thankful that it was true. "I don't need your charity."

He looked taken aback. "Your father changed his mind?"

She lifted her chin. "He did." She'd never admit to anyone in a million billion years that her mother had been behind it.

He smiled at her and butterflies did 360s in her stomach. "I'm glad." He looked at the thick folder. "Who'd he give you?"

She pressed her lips together. "JP Jesse. A free agent wide receiver."

Dominic frowned. "Tom is setting you up to fail."

She couldn't let Dominic know that she'd thought the very same thing. "JP is undervalued."

"He's undisciplined."

"He's uncultivated," she countered.

"He's a troublemaker."

He stood up and walked to the window. "You're smart, Melissa," he said, "and I've been consistently impressed with the work you've done for the agency."

"But?"

He rubbed his smooth chin, carefully weighing his words. "You're green. There's no way you can handle a player like JP the first time out. I'm offering you my help." His eyes bored a hole into her. "Take it."

She stared at him, the way the sunlight surrounded him like a halo. As much as she wanted to deny his statements, he was right. The odds of her failing were enormous. Especially if her first—and only—client was a playboy with a tenuous future.

And yet, she couldn't accept Dominic's offer. Not when he was switching agents for all the wrong reasons.

"I told you this morning and I'll tell you again—I'm not angry," she said in a soft voice. "So please don't feel guilty anymore."

He took a step toward her. "I owe you."

She shook her head. "No, Dominic. Not like this."

He moved closer and she fought the urge to back up. She couldn't think straight when he was near.

Not budging an inch, he said, "Working together is the perfect solution."

"You just said it yourself," she insisted. "I'm green. Why would you put your career in the hands of someone you think can't handle it?"

He closed the distance between them, pulling her hard against him, just as he had in the photo studio. Then his mouth was on hers and he was kissing her like he did in all her dreams, as if he were dying of thirst and she was the only water for miles. At last he pulled away.

"One more time," he murmured as she tried to catch her breath. "You're an amazing woman, Melissa. You can handle anything thrown your way. Even me."

She pressed her fingertips to her mouth. Was that why he'd just kissed her? To see how she'd handle it? The past twenty-four hours had been the most confusing of her life. She could barely think straight now that he'd kissed her again, and she knew that she shouldn't make such a big decision so quickly anyway.

She edged toward the door, picking up JP's folder. "I need some time to think about it."

She could have sworn he was about to smile, that he thought he'd already won. Instead he said, "Fair enough. I'll pick you up at seven."

"What are you talking about?"

Again he closed the distance between them. "I'm taking you to dinner tonight. And we're going to talk. About your career." His eyes fell to her lips, still buzzing from his kiss and utterly desperate for another. His gaze returned to her eyes. "And mine."

Melissa felt dazed. Was this supposed to be a date? Or was this purely business?

Or, worst of all, was it round two of his apology for impulsively having sex with her?

*

It took every mind game Dominic knew to shake off the vision of Melissa in that tight purple sweater. Like one of Pavlov's dogs, he'd been salivating at the thought of tonguing her nipples again, of sucking her sweet flesh into his mouth.

Jesus. He needed to get a grip.

He'd cornered her to make amends, not to fuck her senseless in the McKnight Agency boardroom. He still couldn't believe how calm she'd been this morning. She hadn't even wanted him to apologize for his out-of-line behavior. But his gut had told him he'd screwed up, and he had to fix it. Even if she didn't want him to.

Then he'd lost control again and kissed her. Shit, he hadn't been able to think straight, hadn't been able to concentrate on anything but her luscious curves and her sweet mouth. But the too-short kiss hadn't gotten her out of his system. Instead, he wanted her more than ever, wanted to continue where that kiss had left off.

For twenty years, he'd honed his control on and off the football field. Now was no time to lose it. It was time to put his mistakes behind him and move forward, just like he'd always done.

Bypassing Angie with a kiss on her cheek, he knocked once before walking into Tom's office. As they shook hands and said hello, Dominic studied the successful businessman. He would go ballistic if he found out his daughter was sleeping with a man he trusted. Any man would.

Ever since he'd fucked up big time in high school, he'd made it a point to stay out of the doghouse. No illegitimate children. No bar brawls. No trash talk. Until last night, with Melissa, when he hadn't been able to stop touching her, to keep his dick out of her slick heat.

Not wasting any time on pleasantries, he said, "I hear you gave JP to Melissa."

A flash of surprise crossed Tom's face. "Word travels fast in this business."

Dominic sat across from Tom on the leather couch. He remembered when Tom had been named agent of the year at the Sports Business Awards dinner. That was the year Dominic's endorsement offers had shot through the roof. And Tom had negotiated the hell out of them, making Dominic a very, very rich man.

"JP's gonna be a tough one."

Tom shrugged. "If she drowns in the deep end, it'll be her own damn fault for swimming out too far."

Dominic didn't like Tom's attitude, and his resolve to work with Melissa strengthened. "Move me. Melissa can have both of us."

Tom frowned. "Are you shitting me? Why the hell would you want her to represent you?"

"She's got potential. You're her boss; I'm sure you see it," Dominic added, even though he knew damn well that Tom saw nothing of the sort. "Someone's got to give her a chance. I've been in this business a long time, and I've watched her grow into a hell of a businesswoman. I'm happy to help out."

"Did she beg you to do this? Did she cry?"

"Of course not." Dominic stood up. "Hand her my files."

He left, anger thrumming through his veins. He needed a killer workout to keep him from knocking his ex-agent's teeth out.

Tonight, over dinner, they'd talk business. And then he'd take her home and leave her there. With her doors locked and dead bolted, she'd be safe from him.

Like she should have been all along.

*

"What the fuck is going on between you and Dominic?"

Melissa spun around at the sound of her father's voice. He never swore. Never.

"Follow me," he demanded.

She shot out of her chair and followed him into the same conference room she and Dominic had occupied not five minutes earlier. Her father waited for her to step inside before closing the door. Loudly.

"Dominic just waltzed into my office and told me to transfer his files to you." He pinned her with a hard gaze. "Did you know about this?"

Melissa didn't know what to do. Should she lie? No, she was a terrible liar. It would only make things worse. "Yes," she said. "He wants to work with me. I told him no."

Her father's gaze was unyielding. "You turned down an offer to work with one of the greatest football players of all time?"

She nodded. "I want to be an agent, but I'm not going to steal your clients."

Tom walked past her to stare out the plate-glass windows at the Bay. "Sink or swim."

"Excuse me?"

Her father turned to face her, his expression unreadable. "I don't have the first clue why he wants to work with you. But go ahead, take him. He's yours." He strode to the door, stopping just inside the threshold. "Just be careful, Melissa. Dominic might seem like a nice guy, but he's just like any other player, keeping an eye out for the next best thing to come along." He paused. "And I wouldn't trust JP as far as I could throw him. You're a pretty girl. Don't forget it."

CHAPTER NINE

Early that evening, Melissa spent another hour trying on outfits.

She should have spent the time digging deeper into JP's situation, but too little sleep last night combined with her intense anticipation of dinner tonight made concentration impossible. So far, all she'd done was google JP and print out his long list of transgressions. The press certainly loved writing about all the trouble he got into. The huge stack of gossip pieces and articles awaited her tomorrow morning, along with an appointment with her new client at his oceanfront rental along the Pacific Coast Highway in South San Francisco.

She needed to settle things with Dominic tonight, so then she'd be clear-headed and focused in the morning. The only problem was, she couldn't forget the way he'd made her feel, the way he'd branded every inch of her skin with his touch.

One night with him had changed everything. She would never be able to settle for anything less than the passion he'd aroused in her. Which laid the impossible task before her: find another man who utterly and completely rocked her world.

The doorbell rang and her heart fluttered madly as she headed into her foyer/living room. Her apartment was piddly compared to Dominic's expensive, masculine lair, but it was a cozy place to come home to. She opened the door and lost her breath.

She should have been used to his magnificence by now, but she wasn't. Far from it.

"Come in," she said in as strong a voice as she could manage with no air in her lungs.

He handed her a single rose. A red one. "For you."

He was simply being a gentleman. He probably bought dozens of roses every week for dozens of women. Dominic's thoughtfulness was part of his innate charm. It had nothing whatsoever to do with how he did—or didn't—feel about her.

"Thank you. It's beautiful." Glad to have something to do with her hands, she found a vase for the rose.

His eyes hungrily traveled her body, and she wondered if she was imagining the possession she read in his eyes.

"You look wonderful."

The V between her legs throbbed with need, now that she knew how his touch could turn her inside out in the most pleasurable way possible.

No—she *wouldn't* keep doing this to herself. Crumpling the rose's wrapping into a ball and shoving it into the garbage can, she told herself to stay on track. Strictly professional.

As they walked out to his car, she stuck to business. "What do you think about the team's prospects for next year? Any new players to watch?"

He pulled away from the curb, then turned to look at her. "I have high hopes that we'll win another Super Bowl." And then: "You look beautiful, Melissa."

She turned away and pretended to look out the window. She'd thought they had an unspoken agreement to stick to business from here on out. What was he doing?

A few silent minutes later, they pulled up in front of Cravings, the hottest restaurant in the city. "I've always wanted to eat here," she said, now that there was a safe, utterly unsexy topic at hand. "I hear the wait list is crazy, that they're booked months in advance."

The valet opened her door and helped her out of the car, but Dominic was at her side before the man could help her up to the curb. She was surprised to recognize the very handsome owner standing at the entrance, saying hello to some customers, thanking others for coming. Jason had gained fame as a restaurateur in Napa and had opened this San Francisco location less than a year earlier.

A huge smile lit his face when he saw them, and

he and Dominic embraced before he turned to greet her. "What a pleasure to meet you. I'm Jason."

She was amazed that a truly gorgeous man like him didn't make her heart race. "Melissa McKnight." Wanting to clarify things immediately, she quickly added, "Dominic and I work together at the McKnight Agency."

Jason's friendly expression didn't change. "He'll probably forget to tell you this, but I've kicked Dominic's ass on the football field more than once."

Dominic let Jason's obvious fib go. "I appreciate you squeezing us in last minute."

"Anything for a friend," Jason said as he escorted them through the packed house and into a private, far-too-intimate dining room. "Enjoy your meal."

"Jason seems really nice. Especially considering how good-looking and successful he is."

Something that looked like jealousy crossed Dominic's face. "He's a good guy. Married his college girlfriend recently."

A waiter knocked, then entered to pour two glasses of complimentary champagne.

"I want to know more about you, Melissa."

She hastily swallowed the liquid in her mouth. "Why?"

Dominic's small smile made her hot all over. "I met you fifteen years ago, but we've never really talked."

Because he'd always been a superstar and she'd always been in awe of him. And even though she'd memorized every interview he'd given during the past twenty years, she didn't really know anything about him at all. His prefootball past was vague and mysterious.

Another waiter came in to give them the details of the seven-course menu, and she nodded in all the right places even though she didn't hear a word he said. As the waiter placed an *amuse-bouche* on the plate in front of her, she told Dominic, "My life is very ordinary. I'd rather hear about yours."

"Not everyone finds football exciting." Popping a seared scallop into his mouth, he swallowed before adding, "My mother wanted me to be a doctor."

She smiled. "I remember reading about that in *Sports Illustrated.*"

He grinned. "What else do you know about me?"

Her face grew hot. "Nothing much," she lied.

"No?" he teased.

"It's my job to know about McKnight Agency clients," she insisted.

He merely smiled at her.

"In any case," she said, trying to get their conversation back on track, "your mother must be very proud of you now. You're one of the greatest wide receivers of all time."

Again, his grin told her that she'd said too much.

"Smirking at me is no way to accept a compliment," she said, liking this verbal sparring too much for her own good.

His gaze fell to her lips, then slowly moved back up to her eyes. "Thank you. And yes, she's proud. But she never quite got over my not finishing college, let alone not going to medical school."

Dominic had catapulted into the spotlight after catching a season-winning Hail Mary pass during his sophomore year. The pros had beckoned, and Melissa knew how hard it was for players to turn down millions. Especially a top draft pick, like Dominic. Finishing college was a great goal, but the risk of getting hurt and missing the pros was too big.

"It would have been crazy for you to play college ball. You did the right thing."

His eyes locked onto hers. "A lot of things are crazy. But that doesn't mean we shouldn't do them."

Her nipples grew hard and she bit back a frustrated groan. He probably didn't mean anything sexual by that; it was just her mind playing tricks on her.

The waiter knocked again, then came in with the second course.

Dominic asked her, "Have you always wanted to be an agent?"

As she cut into the spinach and feta ravioli, she nodded. "My father's job always seemed so exciting."

"Is it?"

She smiled. "I love working with athletes. That's why I got my MBA. It was either that or a law degree."

"Smart move. I'd think other agencies would be dying to get you on board."

She bit her lip. She'd been planning that very thing this morning, before her father had offered her JP. And then Dominic.

"All I care about right now is making JP a great deal with a new team."

Dominic smiled indulgently. "Lucky guy."

She blinked, trying to get her feet back on steady ground. "My father went ballistic on me today, by the way. Thanks for that."

Dominic sat back, his muscular frame barely contained by the chair, and took a sip of sparkling water. She'd noticed over the years that he rarely drank, and admired his restraint. Especially since she was gulping down her wine as quickly as it landed in her glass.

"I want to work with you, and your father has no choice but to accept my decision."

She put down her glass. "But I don't. I want to build my career legitimately, not because you or anyone else feels sorry for me."

"I hear what you're saying. But I still think you're making the wrong decision."

She held his gaze. "Wrong or right, it's my decision, Dominic. Not yours."

Something that looked like respect surfaced in his eyes. "Okay then, I guess that means I'm on the hunt for a new agent."

"I hope you'll be happy at another agency."

"The only person I want to work with is sitting right in front of me." His voice was warm and smooth.

"*Why* won't you take no for an answer?"

The way he looked at her turned her insides to jelly. "I've never taken no for an answer."

Arousal instantly flooded her panties. If she hadn't known better, she would have thought he was trying to get back inside her panties! That was utter craziness. He was the one who'd kicked her to the curb, not the other way around.

They ate in silence for several moments, and then Dominic said, "I bought you a gift to seal the deal."

"There *is* no deal," she reiterated, but he'd already pulled out a small velvet bag and put it beside her wineglass.

The delicious food turned to cement in her mouth, and she took a big swallow of wine to force it down. "I can't, Dominic."

"Open it," he coaxed in a soft voice.

She'd been brought up to be polite, no matter

what, and she just didn't have it in her to be surly in the face of an unexpected gift.

Plus, she was dying to see what he'd bought her. Being around Dominic was like sticking to a diet all day long, then stuffing her face with an entire chocolate cake at midnight.

She picked up the small black velvet bag and untied the silk bow around the top, and into her hand fell a string of diamonds alternating with purple sapphires on an intricately woven platinum chain. She sucked in a breath as Dominic rose from his chair.

"Let me."

He gently brushed her hair to one side, then picked up the necklace. Laying the string of jewels between her breasts, he slid his fingers up the chain, along the sensitive skin of her collarbone and neck. She shivered in response.

The necklace perfectly matched the purple cashmere sweater she'd worn earlier today.

CHAPTER TEN

Melissa touched the stones lightly. "Dominic, this is too much. I can't keep it; it's too expensive. Too . . . beautiful," she finished softly.

As she turned to look up at him, her mouth lush and pink and her eyes sparkling, Dominic's hard-on edged against his zipper.

"*You're* beautiful," he said, needing desperately to kiss her, to feel her mouth beneath his, to taste her.

He knelt between her legs to cup her face, tangling his hands in her hair as his mouth found hers. He hadn't intended to seduce her at his friend's restaurant. Just as he hadn't meant to kiss her earlier in the boardroom. Or make love to her repeatedly at his house the night before.

He'd never felt so drawn to anyone before, never needed a woman this badly, never craved her touch beyond reason. But the past eight hours had been a goddamned eternity, waiting to taste her again, and he was rougher than he intended as he forced her lips open with his tongue.

She groaned and instinctively opened her legs so that he could move in closer.

"I want you, Melissa. Right here. Right now."

He'd meant to get her permission to make love to her here, but being with her made him crazy, made everything he intended to say gently sound like a ruthless sexual demand, instead.

She sucked his lower lip between her teeth. "What if someone comes in?"

"We're safe here. If we don't answer when they knock, they'll go away."

"Promise?"

With a groan, he slipped his hands beneath her ass and said, "I promise," before covering her mouth again in a hot kiss. As she wriggled in his palms, his brain shut down as his cock surged.

"All I've been able to think about for hours and hours," he admitted as he pushed back her black silk dress to bare her breasts, "are your perfect breasts."

A sheer black bra barely covered her tight nipples, a sexy showcase for the most gorgeous tits he'd ever seen.

"I kept thinking about doing this," he said, pushing the mounds together with his palms and covering her lace-covered nipples with his mouth. She arched her back as he slid his tongue and thumbs over the stiff peaks.

"And this." He gently nipped at her rosy flesh with his teeth.

"Oh, God," she whispered, "yes."

The final vestiges of his self-control vanished. With Melissa, he couldn't even wait sixty seconds to dip into her honey pot. Being with her made him crazy, made him act like a sex-starved maniac.

Even though it hadn't even been a full day since he'd fucked her.

He slid his hands down her ribs, over her waist, pushing her dress higher and higher as he made his way south. She opened her legs wide and his fingers were greedy in their desperation to touch her, to feel how wet she was, to slide into her.

Her panties were damp, and a drop of precome shot to the head of his dick. He pressed against her fabric-covered mound with the pad of his thumbs, then slipped one finger under the band, and hit gold. Her pussy was slick and smooth. He slid one digit in to the hilt. She bucked into his hand, tightened her grip on his shoulder, and a whimper emerged from her throat.

He couldn't just let her come again with only his fingers. He had to taste her, too, lave her cunt with his tongue until she cried out in ecstasy.

Effortlessly lifting her hips off the chair, he slid her panties off and dived between her legs to lick her pussy in long strokes. She rocked her pelvis into his tongue and he pumped his fingers in and out of her in perfect counterpoint to her swaying hips.

Any second now she would come, and he would be hard-pressed not to blow in his pants. He would barely be able to hold out long enough to slip on a condom and pull her down on his shaft. He wouldn't win any records for staying power, but it didn't matter. All that mattered was giving her pleasure.

And feeling her suck him dry.

Her breath came in short gasps as she climaxed into his mouth. His hands wanted to be everywhere at once: swirling her clit, in her pussy, on her silk-covered nipples. He couldn't wait another second, couldn't wait for her to come down from her climax before he sank into her tight, wet heat. He unzipped his pants, reached into the pocket for a condom, and slid it over his huge erection. A second later, he pulled her off the chair and onto his shaft.

She slid down, taking him inch by sweet inch into her tight hole. They were a perfect fit, and he pushed in deeper until she was rocking into him, pulling his face to hers and kissing him passionately. He knew she was going to come again, close on the heels of her first orgasm, but he could barely think about anything besides his throbbing dick. He wanted to focus on her pleasure, tried so damn hard to concentrate on swirling her clit and squeezing her breasts, but all that did was make him harder, send him closer to his explosion.

His orgasm hit him like a three-hundred-pound linebacker, knocking the breath from his lungs. Melissa's contractions merged with his as they banged against each other on the floor, coming as hard as he ever had. Their mouths were sloppy, biting and licking and kissing and sucking at each other's.

At last she collapsed in his arms, exhausted by the force of their lovemaking. He felt like he was just getting started. He wanted to take her home right now and make love to her all night long.

But less than a minute later, her body language shifted from relaxed to tense. She untangled her limbs from his, awkwardly getting on her feet in the small space between his body, her chair, and the table.

"I need to go to the ladies' room," she said, her words tripping over one another. "Excuse me."

Before he'd even zipped up his pants, she was gone.

CHAPTER ELEVEN

Melissa's alarm went off and she sat up in bed, staring at her puffy face in the mirror over her dresser. She'd barely slept all night, after running out on Dominic in the middle of dinner.

This time he'd seduced her, and she'd been even more out of control than the first time he'd loved her senseless. Anyone could have walked in on them. Anyone could have witnessed her greedily riding Dominic's huge cock for all she was worth. Not only did she have no self-control where Dominic was concerned, she was completely devoid of common sense.

Two hours later, she rang the doorbell of JP's enormous new mansion in the prestigious Sea Cliff neighborhood. A house like his rented well into the double-digit thousands per month, and with no contract, he wouldn't be able to pay for it much longer at that burn rate.

And if she didn't get JP a new deal fast, both of

them would be out on their asses with no job and no money.

A middle-aged woman wearing an apron opened the door. "Well, aren't you a breath of fresh air? Come in. I'll take you to his majesty."

Not sure what to make of that greeting, Melissa followed the woman down the hall to the stairs.

"One floor down, first door on your right." The woman walked off, whistling a pop melody. Melissa headed down toward the blaring seventies rock music.

Knowing a knock wouldn't be heard over the deafening music, Melissa let herself in. Her mouth fell open. JP was pumping iron in a fully equipped home gym with an incredible view of the ocean. A young woman was riding along the sand on a white horse, but even that beautiful picture paled in comparison to the impressive musculature of JP's upper body.

Melissa waited for a tingling sensation to start in her belly and between her thighs—the same inner buzz she got every time she saw Dominic.

Nothing.

Great. Just great. Any other woman would already have whipped off her panties and begged JP to do her. But no, not her.

JP dropped the heavy weight he was holding back on its rack and turned to her with a wide smile. His eyes moved from her face to her breasts to her legs and back up again in slow procession.

"Hallelujah, you are a luscious package. God must have heard my prayers."

JP was as big a playboy as they came, yet there was something likable about him.

"Save it for the press and your fans. And hopefully your new general manager." She held out her hand. "I'm Melissa McKnight. Your new agent."

He dried his hands on a clean towel before grasping her hand. She prayed for a frisson of energy— but nothing.

"I was pretty upset when I found out Tom had fobbed me off on a new agent," JP admitted through perfectly white teeth, his blue eyes beautifully offset by his even tan. "But now I just might send him flowers."

If Dominic had said something like that, she would have blushed, gotten wet, and begged him to take her right there on the gym mat.

With JP, she felt only mild amusement.

"How about you wait until we make a new deal?" she said. "I'll wait upstairs while you get dressed. We've got a lot to take care of this morning."

He waggled his eyebrows. "I like the way you think, pretty lady."

She held up a hand, forcing away a budding smile. "'Melissa' will be just fine from now on, thanks."

She could feel JP's eyes on her ass as she walked out of the room, and she was flattered. But even though he was her age, he was too cocky. Too wild.

Dominic was the kind of man she wanted to be with. Mature. Quietly confident. And so gorgeous, looking at him made her eyes cross.

The next two hours flew by as she quizzed JP on his entire football career, starting from Pop Warner. She didn't ask him about his DUI; she didn't want a confrontation to rule their first meeting. Next time, though, she was going to push him up against a wall and be in his face about his poor behavior.

Every time JP made a pass at her that morning, she deflected it. Had being with Dominic transformed her in some way? She'd never been a target for such magnetic male attention before, especially not from a man like JP, whose looks could kill.

Honestly, it was kind of fun. She wasn't going to encourage him, of course, but a girl was allowed to enjoy feeling pretty.

She drove back to the office with a smile on her face. Although she hadn't seen JP on the field yet, he certainly was a charmer. But charm could take him only so far. He needed to be the real deal to attract a new team, especially given his past off-the-field antics. For the next few hours she was going to hole up in the film room with JP's game tapes. Once she had a handle on the type of wide receiver he was—

whether he had great hands, speed, blocking skills, or, best of all, a combination of all three—she'd make a list of potential teams to woo on his behalf.

From now on, things would start to look up. Not only would she do a kick-ass job with JP, she'd make herself get over Dominic. Maybe she'd take yoga classes or join a book club. And then she'd meet a nice guy who'd fall in love with her at first glance. They'd get married and have babies, and life would be perfectly normal. Boring, possibly, but that was okay. Anything was better than this roller coaster of emotions.

When she took the elevator upstairs, the cute girl behind the front desk squeaked with excitement. "Melissa, I've been dying for you to get back. Someone very special is waiting for you in your cube. Lucky you!"

The music in Melissa's head ground to a screeching halt.

He wouldn't.

He couldn't.

Jenny looked positively starstruck. "Dominic came by again to see you." Lowering her voice to a whisper, she said, "He's so sexy I can't stand it, but don't tell your father I said so. He fires anyone who thinks the players are cute."

Dominic walked around the corner, and Jenny's giggles filled the tense silence. "Oh good, Dominic, you've found her." She looked at Melissa. "He's been waiting over an hour."

"Have a good meeting with JP?" he asked in a voice that was as smooth as butter.

Remembering everything that had happened last night in the restaurant in vivid detail, she croaked, "Yes."

He smiled, moving closer, much closer than she was equipped to deal with. "I'm glad. I'll buy you a cup of coffee and you can tell me all about it."

He knew she couldn't refuse his invitation in front of Jenny, and she forced a smile. "Great."

Jenny beamed at her, clearly thrilled. "I'll answer your line, Melissa. Don't worry about a thing."

Melissa managed to keep her smile intact until the elevator doors closed. "*What* do you think you're doing?" she hissed.

Dominic was all innocence. "Taking a meeting with my agent."

She closed her eyes and took a deep breath, regretting it when she realized how good Dominic smelled. Her eyes flew open again.

"For the hundredth time, I'm not your agent, Dominic."

He nodded. "You're right: not yet. But since I'm currently agentless, I'd like to run something by you, if you can spare me a few minutes."

Melissa sighed. "I need to watch JP's game tapes this afternoon, but I suppose I could have a cup of coffee with you." What kind of danger could she be in, in a bustling coffee shop with dozens of strangers around?

The elevator opened at the garage, and she looked at him questioningly. "We can walk to the Peet's Coffee just around the corner."

"I know," he said, unlocking his car with his remote. "Hop in."

"I agreed to get coffee. Not get in your car."

"If you don't want to give me your opinion on a new business venture, just say the word."

What could she say to that, without sounding like she was afraid of being alone with him? She got into his car.

He pointed out several excellent restaurants on their drive out of Union Square, acting like nothing had happened last night. They wound through various neighborhoods, heading west of downtown into Golden Gate Heights.

"Where are you taking me?" she asked, unable to keep her curiosity at bay any longer.

"We're almost there." He made a sharp turn around a jagged rock face, then pulled into a dirt lot next to a building that seemed to be made entirely of glass. It wasn't a house, but it wasn't an office building, either.

She got out and followed him to the front door. "What is this place?"

He slipped a key into the lock and grinned at her. "It might be my new restaurant."

She blinked in surprise. "You're going to open a restaurant?"

He opened the door and she walked into the light-filled space. The view from the floor-to-ceiling windows blew her away; the Golden Gate Bridge and the Bay Bridge and Alcatraz were spread before her.

"Wow, what an incredible view! I've never seen the city from this vantage point before."

He came to stand beside her, the heat of his body warming up the chilly space. "I agree. But I'm not going to make any final decisions just yet."

She turned to study his beautiful face. "What are you waiting for?"

He looked her in the eye. "You."

She took a step back. He couldn't *say* things like that to her. Not when her brain took off and ran with it, mutating whatever he really meant into what she wanted to hear. She needed to clarify his statement, and fast.

"I'm happy to give you my opinion. But I don't know anything about restaurants."

His eyes were such a deep, rich brown that they were nearly black. It was too easy to get lost in them, and she forced herself to look away. A gleaming silver espresso unit sat on a chipped granite countertop. He followed her gaze and motioned for her to sit down on a folding chair, dusting it off first.

"Try to imagine the place fixed up, full of people."

She settled into the chair as he worked behind the counter, making their drinks. Anyone could see that the building had great energy; all it needed was some TLC. He handed her a small, steaming cup, then sat beside her.

"How'd you find it?" she asked.

"I like real estate. Keeps me busy during the off season, between workouts and charity events."

She studied him over the rim of her cup. "Have you run your idea by your friend Jason?"

Dominic nodded. "He gave it the thumbs-up. But I'm more interested in what you think."

A smile played at the corners of her lips. "Considering I don't know the first thing about opening and running a profitable restaurant, that's just dumb."

"I can't think of the last time someone called me dumb." He grinned. "At least to my face."

She shrugged. "Athletes are some of the smartest people I've ever met. People are just plain wrong when they immediately assume you don't have brains to match your skills." She took a sip of the wickedly good espresso. "You've never given me any cause to doubt your brainpower . . . until now."

Dominic put his cup down on the counter, then gently removed her fingers from her cup and set it next to his. Her heart rate sped up as he scooted his chair closer to hers and reached for her hands. Initially, she'd been cold in the unheated, high-ceilinged room, but now that his large hands covered hers she was enveloped in warmth. And safety. Which was crazy, particularly since Dominic was such a threat to her emotional well-being.

"You're beautiful, you're sexy, you're smart. I value your opinion."

No one had ever said such wonderful things to her. And then he was moving even closer, and kissing her gently on her lips. "You've been on my radar for a long time."

She sucked in a breath, hardly able to believe him. Had he truly noticed her before the night at Barnum's? Or was he just buttering her up for another easy screw?

"I'll bet you say that to all the girls."

His incredible dark eyes held her captive. "I'm saying it to *you*."

She couldn't stop herself from taking what he was offering, even though she knew she would pay for it with her heart.

"You taste like sugar," he murmured against her lips, threading his fingers through her hair, "and coffee beans."

She plunged her tongue into his mouth and kissed him like she'd been wanting to by the elevator, in the office, in the front seat of his car. Dominic was a drug she couldn't resist. His kisses swamped her senses and his hands on her breasts—oh, God, she loved the way he rubbed his thumbs over her aching nipples—sent her reeling straight toward ecstasy.

Every time he kissed her, every time he touched her, he gave her such incredible pleasure. More than anything, she wanted to make him feel as good as he'd made her feel.

She wanted to go down on him and feel his erection hot and heavy in her hands, the smooth head of his penis against her lips. She wanted to taste his arousal on her tongue. Her excitement level ratcheted up another notch as she deepened their kiss. She pulled away, slowly running her hands over his shoulders, down his hard, muscled chest, stopping at the waistband of his jeans.

She undid the top button with steady fingers, feeling incredibly powerful as she dropped to her knees between his legs.

He groaned so softly she barely registered the sound.

"Melissa," he gritted out, his jaw clenched in an obvious attempt at self-control, "you don't have to do this."

She unzipped his pants. "I want to, Dominic. I want to touch you."

His erection jutted out at her even from the confines of his navy boxer shorts. She ran one finger down his hard length and his thick shaft twitched in response.

"I want to taste you," she said, bringing her mouth down onto his fabric-covered shaft.

His cock was so warm. So hard.

So big.

Greedily, she wanted him inside her, just like last night in the restaurant, when she'd ridden him with no inhibitions. But taking him into her mouth and down her throat was no hardship, either.

*

Dominic looked down at Melissa's naughty smile as she contemplated his cock and wondered how the hell he'd gotten so lucky. When he'd headed to the McKnight Agency that morning, he hadn't thought much beyond seeing her again.

And now, sweet lord, she was on the verge of throating him. He gripped the sides of the chair as she wrapped both hands around his hard-on. He closed his eyes to try to get a grip, but it was impossible to shut down the mind-blowing image of his cock in her soft hands, her mouth less than an inch from the tip. Then her tongue lightly swept over him, from the base of his shaft all the way to the throbbing tip.

He was going to come—there was nothing he could do to stop it. Please, God, all he wanted was to feel her suck him into her mouth. She did, and he couldn't stop himself from bucking up, forcing her to take him deeper. Instead of pulling away, she moaned against him, the sound vibrating against his cock.

He couldn't hold back another second. Roaring his pleasure, he shot down her throat in thick spurts, again and again, until his cock finally ran dry.

His heart pumped hard. After all these years of screwing supermodels and actresses, who would have thought that the one woman who could take him apart would be the smart, sexy daughter of his agent?

And now that he'd had her, he couldn't make himself stop.

CHAPTER TWELVE

Dominic pulled Melissa onto his lap and kissed her hard. "You're incredible," he said, raining kisses down her throat, heading for her breasts.

Desperate for her release, she rocked her pelvis against him, shocked to feel his penis grow thick again. He'd just exploded in her mouth and he was ready for more?

"I want to be inside you," he murmured, his breath warm against her earlobe, heightening her already intense arousal. He reached into his pocket for a condom and handed it to her.

"If I didn't know better, I'd swear you were superhuman," she teased.

He kissed her until her head was spinning. "You do crazy things to me."

She ripped open the condom wrapper with trembling hands, then slid the rubber sheath down his impossibly big second erection, and he lifted her over it. She took him in one swift stroke, then rose all the way, until his engorged head emerged slick and throbbing with need. Again and again she slid down, then up, flexing her inner muscles against him, reveling in the potent pleasure of loving Dominic. She'd never come before without direct clitoral stimulation, but she was so aroused by blowing him that she already felt the beginning of an orgasm.

Dominic rocked slowly and patiently inside her, and his steady motions were the final push she needed. She cried out as wave after wave of pleasure came over her, and when he climaxed inside her, his cock throbbing and pulsing in time to her release, she was no longer sure where his body ended and hers began.

They held on to each other forever, it seemed, and Melissa wanted never to let go. She didn't want to have to deal with reality. And she definitely didn't want to hear Dominic apologize again for making her feel so damn good.

The building creaked in the wind, and she jumped. Oh shit. If someone caught her with Dominic, her career could be ruined. How could she be taken seriously if she couldn't keep out of players' beds?

She jumped off his lap and readjusted her clothes, her damp panties a reminder of how strongly Dominic affected her.

"We're safe," Dominic said, instantly assessing her concerns.

"We need to stop having sex in public places."

Damn—she'd made it sound as if she expected their affair to continue in private. And he wasn't interested in another lecture about how they shouldn't even be having sex in the first place.

Dominic ran a hand through his dark hair and said, "I didn't intend to bring you here to seduce you. Again."

She shook her head. "And I didn't mean to let you. But I wanted it, I wanted you." Her lips curved up. "And it was wonderful. All of it."

He looked at her with surprise. "You're not angry?"

She forced a shrug, though she had no idea what they were doing. This was no longer a one-night stand, yet he hadn't stepped up to the boyfriend plate, either. Booty call?

Well, why not? She could have a sexy fling with the best of them. Especially when the man she was flinging with was as incredible as Dominic.

"How could I be angry? You're an incredible lover, Dominic. I'm sure I'm not the first woman to tell you that."

But if she really did want a professional relationship with him, she couldn't keep having sex with him. No matter how good it was.

Escape was the only option. She looked at her watch. "I'm afraid I need to get back to work for some meetings."

Without waiting for a reply, she let herself out the front door and waited in the passenger seat of his car, her heart pounding. She felt unbelievably brave. And desperately out of control.

A couple of minutes later, his footsteps sounded on the gravel outside.

His face was grim when he finally sat behind the wheel, and she could tell by the way his jaw clenched that he was angry. It was good to know that he didn't have any better grip on himself than she had. He sped back down the hill and came to a screeching halt in front of the agency, and she shot out of the car and into the safety of the building.

When the elevator doors opened, Jenny look relieved to see her. "Wow, that sure was a long lunch. I didn't know what to tell JP."

All the blood drained from Melissa's face. "JP is here?"

"He's waiting in the film room. I told him you'd just left with Dominic, but he insisted on waiting for you."

Great. She'd been so busy having sex with Mr. Off-limits that she'd completely ignored her one and only client.

She knocked on the door before letting herself

in. JP was watching himself make a key block on the enormous screen. The lights were off, and even though he was a gorgeous man well known for his powers of seduction, she wasn't the least bit worried about joining him.

He gave her one of his patented "let's have sex" looks, then patted the seat next to him.

He was so different from Dominic. Light where Dominic was dark, full of laughter where Dominic would likely have growled at her instead.

She liked JP.

But she lusted for Dominic.

Enough! JP was going to be the center of her universe from now on.

*

Dominic had never been this far off his game. He couldn't go the distance with Melissa, but he couldn't stay away from her, either. Worse, it wasn't just lust anymore. That first night had been purely physical. But every time he touched her, he fell further into the deep end. He was starting to care too much to lead her on, yet he couldn't leave her alone.

Dominic had learned to control any inappropriate urges long ago. One huge slip-up in high school had taught him that fucking around would never get him where he wanted to be. He needed to keep his distance until his libido cooled down. He'd head to the gym for a long workout, then sit down with his lawyer and finalize the details of taking ownership of his new restaurant.

But everything within him rebelled against the way he'd left things with her. Taking her up to his future restaurant and making love to her again, then telling her he hadn't meant to seduce her—that was the coward's way out.

He'd been a coward once, a long time ago, and it had changed him, changed everything. He refused to be a coward ever again.

Dominic pulled a U-turn in the middle of a busy intersection, barely registering the chorus of honking cars. He was a man on a mission, and five minutes later he dropped his keys into the valet's hand—something he usually never did, with a car as valuable as his—then stopped the elevator doors from closing with his forearm.

Several people muttered their discontent at being held up, but when they realized who he was, their frowns turned to smiles. A couple of women "accidentally" rubbed up against him. It was par for the course, and usually he wasn't bothered by the attention, but this afternoon it irritated him.

He wasn't interested in being a football hero today. He was focused on only one thing.

He pushed through the McKnight Agency's double doors and made a beeline for Melissa's cubicle. She wasn't there. Shit. Jenny ran down the hall toward him.

"Are you looking for Melissa?"

He nodded and her eyes widened.

"Wow, she's really popular all of a sudden."

A surge of possessiveness rose inside him. "How so?"

"Well, first you came and took her to lunch, and then JP came to see her, and now you're back again."

JP Jesse.

Dominic was going to kill the little punk. If he so much as laid a hand on Melissa, he wouldn't live to play another game.

"Where are they?"

Jenny looked surprised by his curt question. But visions of Melissa and JP naked together skipped through his head, and his fists clenched.

"JP wanted to watch some film while he waited for her to come back, and she joined him a few minutes ago."

Fuck. Melissa and JP were in a small, dark room together. Lord only knew what tricks that little prick was trying with her. Dominic didn't know him well—they were of different generations—but he'd heard enough stories. JP was the kind of guy who fucked anything that moved. And Dominic knew firsthand the kind of temptation she presented—even to a guy like him, who usually knew how to keep his dick in his pants.

Tom should never have passed JP off to Melissa. She wasn't savvy enough to defend herself against someone as wily—and charming, not to mention good-looking—as JP. He'd have to do it for her.

Dominic barged into the room without knocking and flicked on the lights.

Both Melissa and JP covered their eyes with their hands.

"What the hell?" JP said as he looked up and saw the large figure in the doorway. "Dominic, dude, turn the lights back off. You're blinding us."

But Dominic was out for blood. Ignoring JP altogether, he faced Melissa. "Do you know what people are going to say when they find out you've been in here alone with JP?"

"I'm his agent, that's what they'll think."

Dominic laughed, a short, angry bark of a sound. "Bullshit. They'll think you're just another one of his floozies, throwing yourself at him."

"Floozies?" JP interjected. "Damn, I haven't heard that word since I was a kid. How old are you, Dom? Fifty? Sixty?"

A low growl emerged from Dominic's throat. "Old enough to know how to conduct my business the right way."

JP shrugged. "I know you think you're her bodyguard, or whatever, but nothing's going on. Yet. So chill out."

Dominic clenched his jaw in an effort to control himself. The "yet" nearly pushed him over the edge. He couldn't be rational right now, couldn't stand the sight of Melissa sitting so close to a good-looking, young playboy.

Being with Melissa had flipped right and wrong around for him, but some things were still clear: He couldn't let her make the mistake of hooking up with a threat like JP.

Instantly slipping into the smooth persona he'd played so well all these years, he said, "I'm afraid I'm going to have to steal your agent away for a while, JP."

For the first time, Melissa looked angry. "I've already *helped* you enough for one day, Dominic."

His gut twisted. She thought all he wanted from her was a quick fuck. She was wrong—at least he thought she was. Shit, his head was playing games with him. What the hell had he been about to say?

"They're breaking ground on the new ballpark in my name this afternoon."

"So?"

"You're my agent. I need you to be there."

JP looked at her. "You're working with him, too?"

She took a deep breath. "I'm thinking about it."

"That rocks, babe. Teams will take you way more seriously if you're also repping Dominic. Even if your daddy-O gave him the boot 'cause he's ancient," he added tactlessly.

Dominic didn't feel the need to defend himself to someone who'd ridden a wave of luck into the pros, rather than skill. He'd already dug his own grave.

But if JP was screwed, so was Melissa. Somehow, he'd have to figure out a way to help JP for Melissa's sake.

"I've heard enough from both of you right now." She pointed a finger at JP. "You may call me Melissa, or Ms. McKnight. Not 'babe.' " Then she got up and stood in front of Dominic, anger etched into her face. "I don't appreciate what you just did," she said in a low voice. "Not at all. But I intend to do my job, and my father already marked the event on my calendar. As his assistant—not your agent."

CHAPTER THIRTEEN

Concentrating on putting together a spreadsheet of teams that might be interested in JP, Melissa was taken by surprise when her father entered her cubicle and sat down on the edge of her desk.

"How are things going with JP?"

She gestured to the growing stack of papers beside her computer. "We've had a preliminary meeting, and I'm researching the best teams for him. I need to watch some game tapes and get a better feel for his playing style. We're meeting again tomorrow morning to discuss immediate, short-, and long-range plans for his career. I'll probably set up a showcase once we've worked through his issues."

"I see." He paused before going into the real reason he'd stopped by. "I still find it hard to believe that Dominic is interested in working with you. Why the hell would he make a choice like that? Especially since it's been perfectly obvious for years that you have a crush on him. I wonder if he feels sorry for you?"

Melissa had never been so insulted. She narrowed her eyes, more than happy to fight back. "Maybe he caught wind of the fact that you think he's an old hack."

Two red splotches rose on her father's cheeks. "You repeated our private conversation to one of my clients?"

"Of course not," she hissed, mad as hell. "But he's a pretty perceptive guy. It wouldn't take much for him to figure out that your attention has waned."

Tom raised one eyebrow, as arrogant as she'd ever seen him. "Do you actually believe you can do his career justice?"

Dominic had been right when he'd said she was green. But she was smart and capable and willing to work her ass off for her clients.

"That's exactly what I intend to do," she stated, more serious than she'd ever been. She *was* going to rep Dominic. And not only would she do his career justice, she'd get some justice of her own. This time next year, when she was the top-earning agent at the McKnight Agency, her father would be eating crow. Logging off her computer, she picked up her purse and stood. "If you'll excuse me, I have an event to attend on behalf of one of my clients."

She'd never walked out on her father; never had

the last word. Until now. God, how she wanted to look back to see if his mouth was hanging open.

Outside, she leaned against the stone wall, closed her eyes, and took several deep breaths.

Baby steps. She'd just stood up to her father and lightning hadn't struck. She opened her eyes. Not only was she fine, she felt better than ever.

A wave of giddiness swept over her. She was an agent with two high-profile clients! Yes, she was scared, but she'd been doing an agent's job for the past couple of years. She knew what the job entailed. Now she just needed to do it.

Stepping out to the curb, she hailed a cab. "DiMarco Stadium, please. Inner Sunset."

The Dominator was now officially her client. Her very own heartbreaking, orgasm-inducing, bad boy of football.

*

Dominic resisted the urge to scan the parking lot again for Melissa. He'd done events like this a million times; he didn't need an agent to hold his hand. Hell, he shouldn't *want* to see her this badly—it had been only a few hours since he'd had sex with her. No other woman had ever insinuated herself into his head—and body—this badly or this quickly.

He was proud of what his success and money had accomplished in the Inner Sunset district of San Francisco. These kids didn't have football teams in their schools because the district didn't have the money for fields, lights, uniforms, or coaches. DiMarco Stadium was just the beginning. He headed up a board made up of some of the biggest local players in the business, along with several dot-com billionaires he'd befriended over the years. Yet his achievement suddenly felt empty.

He was listening to a teacher tell him how excited the kids were about meeting him, when his skin started buzzing. Melissa had arrived. Excusing himself from the conversation, he turned and went to her.

She looked straight at him. There was something different about her.

She looked incredibly confident, almost fierce. And even more beautiful, if such a thing could be possible.

He was tempted to pull her into the new locker room and take her against the bright red metal lockers.

Shit. He needed to shake off the fantasy. But he couldn't get his thoughts straight, couldn't figure out how he would normally have greeted her before they'd starting sleeping together. Not when she smelled so good and looked so amazing.

She broke the silence, saving his ass. "Congratulations on the stadium, Dominic," she said as she looked around at the bright green Astroturf, the gleaming wood stands, the professional lighting. "You're really doing a great thing for these kids. I'll bet we see some great college players come out of here."

God, she was incredible. How long had he searched for a woman who understood his passion for the game? Melissa was so involved in every aspect of football. She had to be, to do her job right. But it was more than that. She was truly interested in doing good with it, too—unlike some agents, who were in it only for a quick buck and would sell a player out to the highest bidder regardless of the reason.

She really did deserve better than him. She deserved the suburban house and the white picket fence. She deserved a guy who came from a solid background like hers.

Not someone who'd nearly killed his best friend.

Not a guy who lived with his past every goddamn day, who kept his secrets hidden like a coward, so they'd never see the light of day.

Dominic's mouth was tight when he finally replied. "They've accomplished a lot so far. I'm pleased."

"It's okay to take some of the credit," she said as she placed a hand on his arm. "It was your money that made all this happen."

Money was the easy part. Being happy—and living right—took work. Still, he wasn't going to take credit for all the work of the many people who had gotten this district stadium off the ground.

The event organizer came by to see if he needed anything, and Melissa introduced herself. "I'm Melissa McKnight, Dominic's agent."

Dominic schooled his face into an expressionless mask until the woman walked away. "When did you change your mind?"

"We need to go sit down on the stage," she said, leading him across the field like a dog on a leash, adding, "This afternoon," as an afterthought.

He wanted to pull her against him, kiss her senseless, and find out what her reason was. But he couldn't do that in front of all of these people. Not *ever*, if he listened to his conscience.

"Working with you will be no different than working with JP," she said in a firm voice.

"Watch your back around him," he warned.

Fire lit her eyes. "Seems to me I should be far more worried about you."

With that, she walked away to introduce herself to other members of his board. Since her father had been in the business for so many years, she knew several of the retired players.

"Melissa," James said, "I haven't seen you in years. You've certainly grown up well." A couple of other guys added their compliments, making her blush.

Dominic saw red. Didn't they realize she was too young for them? Too innocent? They were all married with kids now, but he knew their dirty, fuck-filled pasts.

Silently, Dominic worked out whom he was going to take down first. James had been a middle linebacker, but with his speed, Dominic knew how to make the big guys wish they'd never gotten in his face. He would enjoy taking each of them apart piece by piece. He'd easily find other players to take their places on his board.

Listening to himself, Dominic could see that he was turning into a crazy man. Jesus. How could he expect these guys to act like father figures, rather than horny guys trying to get into her pants or look down her dress, when he couldn't manage it for even thirty seconds?

A dozen teenage boys walked up to their group, and Dominic turned his attention to them. Ultimately, football had saved his life. Without it, he would have been just be another statistic. Another underage drunk driver who'd wrapped his stolen car around a tree because he had no future to live for. Dominic hoped that the year-round football program he was putting together here would help these kids stay out of trouble. Or get them out of any trouble they were already in.

He fell into the familiar rhythm of the locker

room and almost succeeded in forgetting about his ridiculous fascination with Melissa. But not quite. Out of the corner of his eye, he watched her charm every person she talked to. The men drooled; the women wanted to be her best friend.

When the large crowd sat down for the speeches, Dominic made sure that Melissa was seated beside him. Who knew what another guy would try?

She seemed riveted by the speaker, a high-school principal in his early thirties. Rationally, Dominic knew that this guy was her perfect match. If he had an ounce of decency, he would persuade her to go out with the guy.

Instead, it took every bit of control Dominic possessed to keep himself from tackling the man.

He couldn't let anyone else have Melissa. Not some high-school principal, not one of the has-been players salivating over her, and definitely not some hotshot like JP, who would leave her high and dry when he was done fucking her senseless.

CHAPTER FOURTEEN

Melissa sipped a glass of champagne at the reception, with Dominic hovering close to her shoulder. He hadn't let her out of his sight and all but snarled at any man who'd so much as looked her way. She shouldn't have been happy about the way he was acting—if he didn't want her, then why couldn't some other guy make a play?—but she was anyway.

She'd wanted him to pay attention to her for too long to deny herself the thrill of being wanted.

It was time to make a decision. Should she make it clear to Dominic that she was through being toyed with, and make herself step away from the sensual web he constantly wove around her? Or, should she give in to the sheer sensuality of being with him, give in to how much he seemed to want her right now, knowing that nothing long term would ever come of their amazing lovemaking?

The cute principal came over to them, and Melissa smiled. She had a feeling that this was going to be a lot of fun. Especially given the deep frown Dominic was wearing.

"Dominic," the man said, "it's a great pleasure to meet you. I'm Hank Albright. You've done a wonderful thing for these kids."

Dominic grunted something that might have been, "Good to meet you," but to Melissa it sounded more like, "Go away."

Hank turned to her. "I don't believe we've met yet."

She smiled and opened her mouth, but Dominic was faster. "She's my agent. Melissa McKnight."

Elbowing Dominic in his impressively hard stomach, she offered her hand to Hank. "It's lovely to meet you. Your speech was fantastic."

"Thank you." Hank's eyes sparkled. "I really believe in what we're doing here."

She nodded, moving an inch closer to the high-school principal. "Me, too." It was bad of her—she wasn't interested in Hank—but she couldn't resist toying with Dominic. It would do him good to have to work for her attention this one time.

Especially since she'd made her decision: She was giving in to the joy of a no-strings fling with Dominic.

Dominic plucked her half-full glass out of her hands. "Time to go."

She grabbed a full glass off a passing waiter's tray. "See you later, then."

If she hadn't been so suddenly, utterly confident in her ability to wrap Dominic around her little finger—sexually, at least—she would have been shaking in her heels. Because he looked mad. The kind of mad that sent three-hundred-pound defensive lines scurrying out of his way every Sunday.

Amazingly, Hank seemed oblivious to the power plays around him. "How about we find a quieter place to talk?" he asked her, completely missing the look of fiery death Dominic shot him.

"I'm afraid Melissa has to wrap up a contractual detail for me," Dominic said, as smooth as butter. "Maybe some other time."

She turned to Hank. "Could you please hold my drink for a moment? I need to speak with my client. I'll be right back."

Hank nodded, looking between the two of them uncertainly. "Sure thing."

Melissa led Dominic out of the crowded room, out the back door toward the locker rooms. Stepping inside a freshly painted door, she held it open for Dominic. One of her big fantasies had always been to make love with him in a locker room.

Tonight, she hoped to turn that dream into a reality.

Still, she didn't want to make it too easy for him.

"I don't know what you're trying to prove, Dominic, but I'm an adult. I can speak for myself."

The locker room was nearly dark, but for the moonlight coming through the windows above the lockers.

Dominic was only too willing to play along. With his strong arms, he pinned her against the row of red lockers. "I'm listening," he said in a low voice that made her wet all over again.

It took every ounce of control she possessed not to start kissing him, running her hands down his muscular frame.

"Come closer," she said. "I'm only going to say this once."

He moved closer, his hard chest pressing into her aching breasts. "If I want to date someone else, I'll date him. If I want to have a drink with a guy like Hank, I'm going to."

Dominic's eyes were black as they bored into her. "No."

Her heart hammered in her chest. "What gives you the right to say that?"

The pad of his thumb rubbed erotically against her lower lip. "Because I want you."

It rubbed across her jaw. "Because I need you."

It rubbed down into the hollow of her shoulder blades. "Because you're mine."

She shivered with desire.

"I've wanted to kiss you all night. I want to take

you right here with your legs wrapped around me. I want my cock deep inside you when you come."

She couldn't breathe. Her knees were shaking.

"Tell me no," he whispered. "Tell me to go away and I will. It will kill me, but I swear to God I'll leave you alone."

"Stay," she whispered, and his hand curved around one breast, sending shivers through her entire body. Coming up on her tippy-toes, she pressed a soft kiss on his lips. He tasted like champagne and desire.

A low groan emerged from his throat. "I'm not going to be able to take my time," he said, then crushed her mouth beneath his.

His tongue danced with hers as his hands moved down her body. Every spot he touched came alive, and she moved closer to him. His thick erection pressed into her belly, imprinting her with his desire. His palms played with her breasts, but far too quickly they were gone. She wanted them back on her sensitive nipples. One touch, the slightest pressure of his mouth on her breasts, and she'd explode.

But then she felt him pulling up her skirt, his fingers ripping at her stockings.

"I can't wait another second," he said. He quickly unzipped his pants and slipped a condom onto his shaft, and she instinctively wrapped her legs around his waist as he lifted her off the floor. He slid into her in one deep stroke, and her back smacked into the metal locker with a loud clang.

"Dominic," she cried out as his groan of "Jesus" reverberated off the tiled walls and floor, the drum-beat of slamming lockers joining their voices. Again and again he thrust into her, pulling her against him, then taunting her by pulling out to the tip.

He was fucking her harder than he ever had, and she loved every single second of it, loved making him lose control. Her breasts smacked into the hard wall of his chest with every thrust, and she was so glad she'd worn a thin, lace bra. Even deep in the throes of his orgasm, Dominic shifted her so that his pubic bone rubbed against her clitoris, and a power-ful orgasm surged through her.

Dominic's shaft grew bigger and bigger as her muscles clenched at him. She wanted to feel him hot and alive inside her, with no rubber sheath between them, but she'd have to be happy with this. Just as he began to come, she kissed him with every ounce of love in her heart. She'd never be able to say the words aloud, but she couldn't stop her body from speaking the truth.

He held her tightly against him, his rapid heart-beat pounding against hers. "You're coming home with me," he said against her hair. "This doesn't end here."

Oh yes. She longed to spend the night in his bed, wrapped in his strong arms.

A voice in her head tried to warn her, telling her

to think things through, to stop all the touching and kissing and actually talk to Dominic about his feelings. She slammed the door shut on the unwanted voice of reason. She didn't want reason. Lots and lots more loving was all she wanted.

Dominic usually enjoyed meeting fans, hanging with fellow players, and working with kids. But this time he couldn't wait to leave and get Melissa naked in his bed.

Thinking about her lush curves, a new hard-on pushed into his zipper. Good thing he had put his jacket back on.

"Thanks for a great night," he told the organizers. It was all he could do to keep a pleasant smile on his face when he was picturing Melissa in his bathtub, water runninng over her incredible breasts, her head thrown back in ecstasy as he laved her clit with his tongue.

They finally escaped to his car, but Dominic knew he wasn't going to make it all the way home. Fifteen minutes was fourteen and a half too many. He whipped out of the parking lot, driving with single-minded purpose.

Melissa's soft, husky voice wrapped itself around his throbbing cock. "If you're wondering, your house is in the opposite direction."

He shot her a quick glance filled with promise. "I can't wait that long."

As she squirmed in her seat, he remembered how wet her pussy was, how ready she was for him to sink into.

He pulled into a deserted section of Golden Gate Park and turned off his headlights. His black Viper wasn't very roomy, but that was fine. Just like Melissa's pussy: the tighter the fit, the better.

He pushed a lever beside his seat and it slid back several inches.

Melissa watched with a half smile on her face. "Lost?" she asked, knowing damn well what he intended, but wanting to tease him before she climbed on his lap for another ride.

"Turn around," he said.

She blinked in surprise, but did as he'd asked. He unzipped her skirt, and together they slid it to the floor of the passenger seat. Her panties were still in his jacket pocket, and her sweet pussy was still bare and slick. She was his for the taking, but he wanted her naked first. Her sweater came off next, leaving only her bra. In the dark, he searched for the clasp along her back.

"It's in the front," she whispered, trembling slightly.

He smiled against her neck, then kissed her warm skin. She tilted her head to the side to give him better access. His fingers itched to touch her nipples and he slowly ran his hands over her rib cage, under the soft swell of flesh, finally covering her breasts with his hands.

While one hand undid her bra clasp, the other made its way down into her damp pubic hair, immediately locating the hard nub of her clitoris.

He wasn't the only one dying to fuck again.

"Dominic," she whispered as she opened her legs wider so that he could rub his hand against her plump, aroused pussy lips.

Without warning, he lifted her over the stick shift and pulled her onto his lap. Her back was pressed against his chest, her juicy breasts filling his hands.

"What are you doing?" she asked in an excited whisper.

"Trust me," he replied, more insane over this woman's body than he had ever been before in his thirty-six sexually charged years.

His cock was nestled between her butt cheeks and he caught her nipples between his thumbs and forefingers, teasing the stiff peaks until her wetness seeped into the fabric of his pants. One hand still playing with her breasts, he slid the other between her slick pussy lips, slipping and sliding against her clit, her tight, hot passage. She moaned and rocked her hips rhythmically against his hand, inflaming him with every thrust of her lush hips.

Forcing himself to pull his hand from her pussy, he grasped her hips and lifted her enough to pull down his zipper. He ripped open the condom wrapper with his teeth and slid it onto his throbbing shaft in a move that spoke of years of experience in non-standard positions. But every woman who had come before Melissa was long forgotten.

He didn't waste one more second slipping the head of his cock between her lips, and she moaned with satisfaction. "Dom," she begged, using his nickname for the first time, and his cock surged against her slick folds.

He nearly plunged all the way forward, high and deep, but he wanted to tease her, to work her back up to a fever pitch before finally giving them both the ultimate pleasure.

"Not quite yet, sweetheart," he growled as he replaced his cock with his fingertips.

He'd make sure that she'd never forget tonight. And it was a long time until morning.

CHAPTER FIFTEEN

Melissa was on fire, the blood in her veins like molten lava, her skin sensitive to the slightest touch. The leather steering wheel chafed her nipples; the stick shift scratched her thighs. His fingers played with her clit even as the head of his penis rubbed deliciously against her aroused flesh. She pressed her ass into his hips, but he was still toying with her. Only giving her one finger, and then two.

She whimpered, loving the way he touched her, but craving so much more. She wanted his thick cock to spread her wide again, to fill her all the way up.

She'd never find another man like him, never find someone who made her feel so good, whose body fit hers so perfectly. This knowledge made her throat clog with emotion.

She was his—all his. No matter how hard she tried to resist him, she went off like a rocket at his slightest touch. She could never love anyone the way she'd always loved him—and always would.

Her toes tingled, heady vibrations moving quickly past her ankles to her calves. Oh, God, she was coming again. Only this time Dominic was forcing her entire body to submit to his power.

His cock replaced his fingers so skillfully that it wasn't until she backed into his lap that she realized he was filling her, and she started to come.

"God, Melissa, you feel *so* damn good."

Knowing how much he wanted her, his hands everywhere at once, sent her to an even higher peak. And then she was twisting around in the tiny driver's seat, desperate to kiss him. As his mouth consumed hers, she finally exploded over the edge. Dominic held her hips against his as he shouted out his pleasure, and her inner muscles clenched and pulled against his huge erection.

She wanted to laugh with joy; she wanted to sob. She didn't know what to say, what to do; being with Dominic had stripped her of her last defenses.

A loud banging on the roof of the car made her jump with alarm.

Her limbs were heavy from their explosive lovemaking, and she awkwardly scrambled off his lap, practically falling headfirst into the passenger seat, her butt sticking up in the air, and dug for her clothes on the floor.

"Don't worry," Dominic said as he calmly handed her her bra, then her skirt and top. He rubbed away a streak of lipstick on her cheek. "Everything's going to be fine. Let me handle this."

Dominic turned his key in the ignition and rolled down the fogged-up window. A very stern policeman stared in at them.

"Good evening, Officer," Dominic said in an even tone.

"It's awfully late, folks," the officer said, clearly ready to read them the riot act. Then he realized who his offender was, and his expression instantly changed to one of hero worship.

"Dominic DiMarco?"

Dominic smiled. "We were just heading home," he said. "Sorry to have disrupted your evening."

The policeman waved his hand in the air. "No problem. Just remember, in the future this isn't the best place to score."

Dominic nodded, already raising the window back up. "Thanks. Have a great night."

"Oh, God," Melissa said as he drove away. "That was too close for comfort. If it got out that I was sleeping with a client, I'd be a laughingstock."

He didn't say anything, and the silence grew awkward. Had she hurt his feelings? No, that was impossible. She was as much his secret as he was hers.

Wanting things to go back to the way they'd been

before, she teased, "You were pretty smooth there. How many times have you been caught in a car with your pants down?"

A muscled jumped in Dominic's jaw. "My past mistakes have nothing to do with us. I was just a stupid kid."

Mistakes? What mistakes? She stroked his arm, joking, "Okay, then, how about I tell you about all the sex I've had with guys in cars?"

Dominic hit the brakes hard at the Stop sign. Then gripping the stick shift so hard that his knuckles turned white, he shot forward on the dark, empty road. "I want to rip them all limb from limb," he growled. "Use their faces as punching bags."

It was all she could do not to giggle with glee. "That's not very nice."

"Where you're concerned, I have trouble being nice." He pulled into his parking garage. "I've never wanted anyone as badly as I want you."

"Would it make you feel better if I told you you're my first in a car?"

"I hate thinking of you with other men at all. It drives me crazy."

She tried to keep her feelings in, but couldn't. "You're the only one who matters."

CHAPTER SIXTEEN

S pend the night with me, Melissa."

Melissa let him thread his fingers through hers. "You make it hard for a girl to say no," she whispered.

He smiled at her, a seductive flash of white teeth and stubble dusted across a strong jaw. "I'll keep that in mind." He came around to her side of the car and helped her out just as her stomach grumbled.

"I'm starved, too," he said. "Have you ever eaten spaghetti alla carbonara?"

She shook her head. "My people walked off the *Mayflower*. I grew up on Wonder Bread and processed-cheese slices. Kraft macaroni and cheese, if my mother really wanted to spice things up."

He grinned. "Looks like it's up to me to educate your palate."

They took the elevator up to his condo and

she followed him into his kitchen. Most men she'd been with didn't know the first thing about cooking. They always expected her to whip up something amazing with fifteen minutes' notice. Unfortunately, cooking wasn't part of her skill set. She even burned microwave popcorn. If Dominic could actually cook, it would be one more plus to add to his already long list.

He uncorked a bottle of red wine. "You prefer merlot, don't you?"

She nodded, warmed by the fact that he'd noticed. She sat on a leather bar stool and he slid a glass to her across the black granite island. "White wine makes my toes itch," she admitted.

He raised an eyebrow. "Also good to know."

Butterflies hatched in her belly as she wondered what exactly he was going to do with that knowledge. She wiggled her toes as he pulled out eggs and bacon from the stainless-steel fridge and spaghetti from the pantry. Then he grabbed a pot from the gleaming copper rack above the gas range.

"Where did you learn to cook?" she asked.

"My mother could make anything. She was passionate about food." He reached into the fridge, turning his face away from her. "If cooking shows had been invented thirty years ago, she would have been a star."

Melissa digested this information, wondered

about what he wasn't saying. "Was she a full-time mom?"

He put on water to boil. "My dad died when I was three. She supported us by bagging groceries at the mom-and-pop store around the corner."

Melissa suddenly remembered a story she'd read about Dominic. After signing his first major-league contract, he'd bought his mother a house.

"Were you the youngest?"

"Nope, the oldest. My sister is one year younger, my brother just behind her."

"My God," she said. "Three kids under three. How did your mother do it?"

He looked uncomfortable. "It was rough at times. She did the best she could."

Clearly, Dominic didn't want her to probe any deeper. It hurt her feelings that he wouldn't share with her, but at the same time she understood. She wasn't exactly offering up tidbits about her relationship with her father. Besides, she knew Dominic. He was a natural protector. Were it not for his size, he would have been a natural defensive player.

As a child, he must have tried to assume the role of man of the house. What a big burden that must have been for such a little boy.

It wasn't unusual for pro athletes to have a chip on their shoulders. So many of them had overcome bad childhoods, rough neighborhoods, little money.

But Dominic had never once tried to use his upbringing as an excuse for bad behavior. He was a better man than that. It was one more reason to love him—one more reason she didn't need.

Dominic looked like a wild gypsy with his dark hair, dark eyes, and dark skin. She wanted desperately to be the mate he would sacrifice everything for. But the truth was that there would come a day when she would see another woman giving him a celebration kiss after a game; maybe even pregnant with his child.

Suddenly, Melissa hated that woman with a passion.

She gulped her wine, wishing they could stop talking and get back to bed, where things were simpler. When they were making love she could concentrate on her body and temporarily forget about her heart.

*

Dominic never shared family stories with anyone. Not his teammates, none of his coaches, and certainly none of the women he'd dated. Even his brother and sister avoided rehashing their childhoods when they got together, stepping around the fact that their widowed mother had brought home a new guy every month, and that each guy had been more horrible than the last, until she married the biggest asshole of them all.

His siblings had never thanked him for protecting them from these men; they didn't need to. Someone had had to start making good decisions in their house, because his mother hadn't been able to manage it. So, Dominic had stepped in.

Then, when he was a senior in high school, his mother chose her dick-wad husband over her kids, and Dominic had thought, *Fuck it*. He drank and he fucked and he stole cars. He was a hot-shot football player, the big man on campus with a fancy football scholarship to the University of Miami. He was the master of the drunk joyride with a pantyless girl sitting next to him, writhing beneath his fingers on her clit.

But his lucky breaks had ended late one night just before graduation. Joe had stolen the car, but Dominic was driving. Going a hundred miles an hour made the uncapped bottle of Jim Beam splash onto the leather seats. It was raining and dark, and Dominic had thought he was unstoppable.

The tree knew better. The tree was stronger than both of them, crushing Joe's legs.

Though Dominic walked away from the crash physically unscathed, he was emotionally destroyed. Joe lost his scholarship and never played football again. Dominic should have been prosecuted, should have been made to pay for what he'd done. But Joe's family was big in politics in Washington State, and they had insisted on keeping the incident completely under wraps.

Which was where the official story began. Dominic went to college, went pro, made millions. But every day, he paid for that lack of control twenty years ago. Being with Melissa was the closest he'd come to losing his grip in all that time.

Plating their pasta in silence, he carried their dishes into the dining room.

Melissa took one bite and her eyes grew big. "Dominic! This is amazing. You could give your friend Jason a run for his money."

"I'll pay you to say that next time you see him."

She glanced at him in surprise.

Shit. He needed to watch himself around her. He didn't make women promises, and doing so now was out of the question.

Time to change the subject to something that involved less talking and more fucking.

He pushed his plate away. "I've been thinking."

She put her fork down. "About what?"

"All the jets."

She looked confused. "Jets?"

He nodded. "In my bathtub."

Melissa took a deep breath, and he enjoyed watching her breasts rise. "And?"

"I want to see them in action." He stood up and held out his hand. "With you in the tub."

She took his hand. "And you?"

"And me."

He kissed her softly, and they headed for the bathroom, where he turned the faucets on.

"I've never undressed you," he noted quietly.

She smiled. "There usually isn't time."

He laughed. Sex and laughter had never gone together before, only with Melissa. "That's because I'm a greedy bastard," he said as he reached for the hem of her very sexy silk top.

"No complaints here," she murmured as she lifted her arms over her head.

He admired her nearly sheer lace bra with barely contained lust. He wanted to press her against the tiled wall and do a repeat of their first time together.

"You're too good for me," he said as he put his hand on her back and arched her breasts into his waiting mouth.

Her soft moan drove him crazy, as did the tender way she caressed his back with her hands. Instead of yanking up her skirt again, he reached for the zipper. The skirt fell to the floor and he rubbed his hands over her bare ass, all the while sucking her breasts.

He lifted her in his arms, and a moment later they were in the tub, her back to his front.

"I'm still wearing clothes," she said, lifting one garter-clad leg out of the water. Her lace-covered nipples floated into his palms.

"I did my best," he said, running kisses down her neck.

"There's always next time," she said.

"And the time after that," he agreed, unable to go one more second without touching her pussy. He slid his hands between her legs and she bucked into his hand as he delved into her.

"I can't get enough of you," he said, plunging two fingers in deep. His elbow hit the button that controlled the jets, and they were enveloped by tiny bubbles shooting at them from all directions.

"Open your legs, sweetheart." He rubbed his thumb in slow circles over her clit.

Her thighs moved apart and he urged, "Wider." Putting his hands on her hips, he positioned her in front of a jet. "Tell me when it feels good."

She gasped. "It feels good now. Oh, God!" she said. "*So* good."

"Come for me."

He undid the clasp of her bra and cupped her wet breasts. She moaned with pleasure as he toyed with her nipples and he couldn't stop himself from rubbing his erection into her soft, round ass. His cock was rock-hard and ready to explode as he kissed her neck.

She was breathing heavier, faster, and then suddenly her cries of pleasure were echoing off the walls. Dominic made sure to keep her clit directly over the jet, but as soon as her climax subsided he rammed his cock into her to the hilt. She floated above him in the water as he rocked her up and down on his shaft. He hadn't thought to bring in a condom, and it was going to kill him to pull out.

At the last second he pushed her away, rubbing himself on her soft skin, squeezing her breasts, biting into her neck as he came into the water.

When his heart rate returned to normal, Dominic helped Melissa out of the tub, wrapped her in a towel, and carried her to his bed. She was nearly asleep by the time he pulled the covers over her.

From sunup to sunrise, he'd fucked her four times, none of them in a bed. She deserved her rest.

CHAPTER SEVENTEEN

When Melissa woke up in Dominic's bed, she instantly knew it would be far too easy to get used to sleeping there. How was she supposed to keep her guard up when he was everything she'd ever dreamed of and so much more?

He lay on the living-room floor doing sit-ups in a T-shirt and shorts, and her mouth watered. He wore headphones and hadn't heard her come down the hall, which gave her the opportunity to stare. Would she ever get used to looking at him? His thighs and calves were well muscled and taut as he pushed through his set.

He opened his eyes and grinned at her, slipping off the headphones. "Good morning."

Her stomach somersaulted like she was a teenage girl. "Hi," she said, getting a glimpse of the clock on the wall. Ten-thirty a.m.? "Is your clock right?"

"You were tired."

She blushed. Anyone would have been tired after that many mind-blowing orgasms. "I'm going to be late to work. And you have practice."

He stood up and walked over to her. "Kiss me."

She immediately complied, going up on her tippy-toes. His mouth was warm and intoxicating and she was panting by the time he ended the kiss.

"I'll drop you off at your apartment on my way to the gym. Are you attending the charity event tonight?"

She nodded and he smiled. "Good."

She was beginning to understand what that wicked gleam in his eyes meant. Somewhere, somehow, at the event tonight he'd be pushing her skirt up to her waist and taking her. The anticipation was already killing her.

Ten minutes later he kissed her long and hard in front of her apartment. "If I didn't have practice, I'd be fucking you on your kitchen table right now."

She forced herself to step away from him. Players were heavily fined for skipping practice, so he couldn't stay, no matter how badly she wanted him to.

"Don't bother wearing panties tonight," he said, then left.

Great. She was already wet and burning for him, with a whole day to get through before she could get any relief.

By the time she'd showered and dressed, it was time to meet her best friend for lunch. Alice owned her own recruitment firm and Melissa greatly admired the way she'd built the company into one of the top firms in San Francisco in five years. Focusing on retraining highly qualified women who were getting back into the workplace once their kids were of school age had quickly given Alice a unique edge. Alice claimed that ex-stay-at-home moms worked harder and faster than any man ever could.

Melissa suddenly imagined herself rocking a blue-eyed baby with Dominic's dark hair and skin.

Oh, God, when was she going to accept the truth? Not only was she not going to have babies with Dominic, she probably wasn't going to share his bed for much longer. Everyone liked novelty, Dominic was no different. He was attracted to her only because she was so different from the standard football groupies. But that didn't mean his attraction would last.

Arriving fifteen minutes early at the Pier 39 restaurant, Melissa ordered a glass of wine and watched the tourists as she sipped it. Happy couples abounded. Young mothers chased toddlers; fathers held video cameras. It was all so normal.

And so out of reach.

Alice walked in, reed thin, wearing impossibly high heels, a red sweater, black slacks, and a funky pair of black glasses with red flecks in them.

She wasn't a typical beauty, but there was something intriguing and sensual about her. Melissa had watched dozens of men try to latch on to Alice and fail miserably; Alice wasn't the girlfriend type.

"Honey," Alice said after they hugged, "I don't even need to ask how you are. You're glowing. Whoever he is must be incredible in the sack."

Melissa nearly choked on her wine. "Good to know I'm so transparent."

"Do I know him?" Alice asked.

Melissa shook her head. "No. At least I don't think you do." She cleared her throat and added in a much softer voice, "Although you might have seen him on TV. Or in some magazines."

Alice turned to the nearest waiter. "We're going to need a full bottle." She refocused her attention on Melissa. "You didn't sleep with one of the Outlaws, did you?"

Alice didn't have a very high opinion of football players, even though Melissa was pretty sure she'd never been to a game. Melissa's guilty face gave her away.

"His name?"

Melissa looked at her friend. "You won't know who he is, what does it matter?"

"It matters because that way I can hunt him down and kill him if he ever treats you badly."

"Dominic is a good man," Melissa instantly defended him.

Alice tapped one manicured nail on the frame of her glasses. "Dominic. Hmm, that rings a bell. Is he tall, dark, and handsome?"

Melissa giggled. "You've just described half of the team."

"Are you in love with him?"

Melissa closed her eyes. "I don't know," she lied. "I don't think I should be." She opened her eyes. "I'm not sure it matters either way. He's not the marrying type."

Alice topped up their wineglasses. "How soon can I meet him?"

One of the things Melissa had always admired about Alice was her ability to make quick decisions. Melissa liked to mull over things to death, shred her worries to pieces in her mind until she was left with nothing but pulp. Introducing Alice to Dominic was too risky. It would mess with her plan to bury her head in the sand and enjoy all the naughty sex until he found someone else and the decision was taken from her.

On the other hand, what if Alice saw something she'd missed? Maybe Alice's impartial eye was exactly what she needed.

"There's a charity event tonight at the new aquarium," she said. "I suppose you could come with me. I'll have a client with me, though—another football player. So you'll have to promise to be on your best behavior."

Alice smiled, a wicked glint in her eye. "Hell, if sleeping with a football player will make me look half as good as you do right now, I'll be extra nice."

✳

Summer passing camps were usually a vacation from the grueling practices during the season, and Dominic always enjoyed the chance to hone his skills.

Not today. He'd never fumbled so many balls, never lacked chemistry with the quarterback like this. Dominic poured a bottle of water over his head, trying to drown out the inner voice that said he was screwed, that sleeping with Melissa had jinxed him in some way, had stolen his mojo.

Ty waited until everyone else had left the field before razzing him. "She anyone I know?"

Dominic went still. "Just getting old." For once, he was glad to use his age as an excuse.

Ty didn't buy it. "Took me a while to get my game back on after hooking up with Julie. Don't fight it, man. It'll happen." He gave Dominic a knowing grin. "And let me know when we can meet the woman who finally fucked up your game. She's got to be pretty amazing." He headed into the locker room.

Several Outlaws swore by their "no sex before a game" superstition. Dominic had never noticed it mattering one way or the other, but maybe that was because none of those women had mattered.

✳

Six hours later, Melissa smoothed down her strapless dark-purple dress in the passenger seat of Alice's car.

"You look great, girl. Loverboy's eyes are going to pop out of his head."

"Thanks," she said to her best friend, "but please don't call Dominic loverboy ever again."

Alice grinned. "I did a little research when I got back to the office. He did those Calvin Klein commercials for a while, right? They call him the Dominator?"

"He did." Melissa's face flushed. "And they do."

"No wonder you're so messed up over him. He has phenomenal abs."

They had arrived in Golden Gate Park just as the party was getting under way. Melissa had instructed JP to meet her by the fountain at 6:15 p.m., and prayed he wasn't getting into trouble. She'd stab him with her heel if he was.

Alice took in all the muscles, the gorgeous faces and bodies in their tuxes, and shook her head. "I can't believe I'm actually at this party. Although I certainly wouldn't kick a couple of these guys out of my bed for eating power bars."

Melissa grinned, seeing the world she'd inhabited her whole life with new eyes, realizing for the first time that she'd been taking it for granted. She instantly spotted Dominic across the room, deep in conversation with a top cancer-research specialist Melissa had met at a previous gala. She tried hard to turn a critical eye on Dominic, but it was no use. She couldn't find a single thing wrong with him.

JP walked into her line of vision. "Hey, boss," he said before turning the full wattage of his charm onto Alice, who had bucked the dress code by wearing black leather jeans and a slinky sequined top rather than a cocktail dress.

"Has anyone ever told you what a breath of fresh air you are in a stuffy room?" he said to Alice.

Alice adjusted her black-rimmed glasses. "No," she told him before turning back to Melissa. "Thank God it wasn't him," she said. "I would have seriously doubted not only your judgment but your sanity as well."

Melissa's heart raced. "Not here," she hissed.

JP watched the interaction with fascination. "The day I understand the way a woman's mind works is the day I'm going to start batting for the other team."

Alice faked a sweet smile. "You mean more often than you already do?"

His obvious surprise was cut short by a slow grin. "I'd ask you to marry me, babe, but we both know it wouldn't last. How about a drink instead?"

Alice shrugged. "What the hell. Maybe I can rack up some charity points myself tonight by teaching you how to read."

Melissa bit back a laugh as they headed to the bar.

Dominic looked up, their eyes locked, and she suddenly felt hot. She wasn't wearing any lingerie under her dress. Could he tell?

A photographer from the *Chronicle* came by to say hello, but the bare minimum of Melissa's attention was on their conversation about the upcoming football season. The rest was on every one of Dominic's movements, the way his hair had grown a bit long and was falling over his left eye, the fact that he was still watching her from across the room and his gaze made her warm and tingly all over. Eventually the conversation made its way around to her, and the fact that she was responsible for two new clients.

The photographer's face lit up when she told him who the two players were. "Let's get a shot of the three of you."

Dominic and JP sold papers; they really didn't need her in the picture. But it was a good opportunity to solidify her public standing as a new agent with serious prospects.

She located JP and Alice standing beside the bar, deep in conversation. What would the two of them have to talk about? The fact that they hated everything about each other?

"Sorry to interrupt," she said, "but I need you and Dominic for a quick photo, JP."

"Sure thing," he said, "But are you sure you want to make Dominic look bad by putting the two of us together?"

She fought the urge to roll her eyes. Alice didn't.

"One day, if you're lucky—and have lots of fantastic plastic surgery—you'll look half as good as Dominic," Alice taunted.

But JP just grinned. "Your version of foreplay is hot."

The four of them headed toward Dominic.

"Dom," JP said, "time to take pics with Melissa. You'd better go fix your makeup."

Dominic's hot gaze swept Melissa's face, then he turned to the photographer, ignoring JP completely.

"How's life with the new baby?" he asked, and Melissa noticed the bags under the man's eyes. How did someone as important and famous as Dominic manage to know the small details about the people all around him? Impressed, she vowed to learn from his example.

"She's great," the man said. "My wife and I aren't getting any sleep, but she's worth it."

Dominic looked uncomfortable. Was it because she was standing there amid talk of wives and children? Did he know she'd been dreaming of having his babies?

Melissa took a step back, accidentally knocking into a waiter's tray, and cold, wet liquor seeped into her dress.

Alice quickly took charge. "We'll be right back," she told everyone, then linked arms with Melissa and pulled her to the women's restroom.

"Loverboy," Alice said, "is desperately in love with you."

CHAPTER EIGHTEEN

Hope warred with confusion inside Melissa. "You're mistaking desire for love," she protested.

They locked themselves into a large, private bathroom, where Alice grabbed a wad of paper towels and pressed them to Melissa's back. "No. He loves you."

"Oh really? Then how come the morning after our first time together, he told me how sorry he was? And that we could never make the mistake of sleeping together again?"

"But you have slept together again. Lots of times, right?"

Melissa's face flamed. "It hasn't changed anything. I can tell he still feels guilty, like he would stop sleeping with me if he could."

"Poor stupid bastard—trying to fight the obvious."

Melissa shook her head. "You don't understand.

He's not interested." Alice snorted, and Melissa clarified: "Not in any kind of long-term way. Yet every time I tell myself to stay away from him, the next thing I know my legs are wrapped around his waist."

"No kidding. We were all getting a contact singe out there."

Melissa sat on the closed toilet seat and put her head in her hands. "I don't know what to do."

Alice reapplied her lipstick in the sink mirror. "Have you tried talking with him? You know, duct taping him to a chair on one side of the room so he can't jump you, and asking him some tough questions?"

Melissa raised her head. "No. I already put myself on the line once and got an emotional smackdown. I'm not interested in setting myself up for another big fall."

Her friend looked stern. "If it were me, I'd rather break my own heart than let some guy do it for me. Even if the guy *is* impossibly hot."

"It's just a fling," Melissa repeated. "No strings attached. When it's over, we'll both go our separate ways with no recriminations."

Alice gave her a look that said she was full of it. "You just keep trying to tell yourself that. Maybe one day you'll believe it."

A loud knock sounded on the door. "If you're not dead in there, could you open up before I pee on the floor?"

"You want me to deal with her?" Alice said in a scary voice.

"No. Let's get out of here. I've got an important photo op waiting."

Dominic kept a respectable, professional distance from her as the photographer took dozens of shots. But his eyes followed her around the aquarium the rest of the night as she networked with players, agents, sportswriters, and the coaching staff.

How could he make her so wet with nothing but a glance? He hadn't touched her, yet she was as hot for him as she'd ever been. Maybe even more so, given the hours of anticipation. When was he going to make his move? The waiting was killing her.

Then she thought, what if she propositioned *him* tonight? What if she was the one who did the dragging into a dark corner, rather than being dragged?

A small smile played around the edges of her mouth. That was exactly what she'd do. Now the only question was, how?

Dominic looked to be deep in conversation with the general manager of the Outlaws across the room. But Melissa knew better: He was keeping tabs on her. He would notice if she left the room.

Beyond the newly finished entrance, the aquarium was still a construction zone.

Melissa grabbed a glass of champagne from a passing waiter and headed for the back corner, near a door marked CONSTRUCTION CREWS ONLY. Without so much as a glance behind her, she pushed the door open. Ah, just as she had hoped: a completely deserted space. The walls and roof were on, but it was mostly bare plywood here.

She sipped from her glass, her heart skipping. It wouldn't be long now. And then she heard the faint squeak of the door hinges. She waited a beat, letting him move closer before she turned around.

"Decided to take a tour?" he asked, his deep, sensual voice washing over her.

She set her glass on a stack of Sheetrock. "I couldn't wait any longer."

"I was feeling exactly the same way."

She walked into his arms, and as he slid one hand over her ass, she shivered with excitement.

"I don't feel any panties but I'm not sure I can trust my hands."

His fingers found her zipper, and as he began sliding her strapless dress off, her legs started trembling. A moment later, she was standing nearly naked in front of him, wearing only garters, heels, and the beautiful necklace he'd given her.

A growl emerged from his throat. "Sweet lord, you're beautiful."

No one had ever looked at her like he did—like he was the luckiest man in the world. She felt impossibly beautiful in his eyes.

He was already kneeling in front of her, his breath hot on her clit. His hands came around her hips, holding her upright for his sensual invasion. His tongue found her first, warm and so knowledgeable about the perfect way to make her come. He didn't bother teasing her, since the whole night had been foreplay, but licked her with long, smooth strokes from her labia to her clitoris. The orgasm came before she was even aware of it.

The next thing she knew, she was in his arms and he was carrying her across the room. He took off his jacket without putting her down and laid her on a table, cushioned by the black fabric. She reached for his zipper but he was two moves ahead of her, his sheathed cock ready and waiting for her to take it in.

"All night long I've wanted you," he said. "Every goddamn second. You're so sweet, Melissa. So perfect."

He drove into her, his kiss rough and possessive as he claimed her, and she took him deeper, wishing this moment would never end.

She was his. Forever.

✳

What the fuck am I doing? Dominic asked himself thirty minutes later, when he and Melissa were back out mingling on opposite sides of the room. Things were getting out of hand.

One accidental fuck could easily be accounted for, especially considering how long he'd wanted her. But instead of getting her out of his system, each time they had sex he wanted her more. Anyone could have walked in on them in the construction zone. They'd gotten lucky. Again. He couldn't count on that luck forever.

In fact, part of him wanted the chance to come clean. To tell the world that she was his woman. *His.*

Shit. Now wasn't the time to think about that. Not when all he could think about was taking Melissa home and making love to her all night long.

Out of the corner of his eye he watched her leave. If he'd had any self-control, he would have let her go home to her apartment alone and get some sleep.

Forcing himself to do his duty as an Outlaw, he socialized awhile longer, then extricated himself from the party. His cock was rock hard and he broke a dozen traffic laws getting out of Golden Gate Park. He passed the parking lot where she'd ridden him doggy-style, and a drop of precome emerged on the head of his dick.

At this rate, he wasn't even going to make it to her place. He raced up her steps and rang her doorbell, feeling like a kid on Halloween, with Melissa as the candy.

The building door buzzed open, and when he got to her apartment door he barely let her open it before his mouth was on hers and he was kissing her as if he hadn't seen her for weeks.

When he finally let her catch her breath, she said, "I was just putting together something to eat. I thought you might be hungry."

He nodded, following her into the kitchen, one hand threaded through hers. His stomach growled, but it would have to wait.

She looked up at him. "That was pretty wild tonight, wasn't it?"

He nodded, forcing himself to reply, trying not to be such a sexed-up ogre. "Wild."

"I can't believe we did that," she said, and it finally occurred to him that she looked nervous.

He pulled her against him. "It was incredible. You're incredible."

She pressed a kiss to his lips and whispered, "Remember what you said to me this morning?"

He looked into her amber eyes. "About fucking you on the kitchen table?"

She nodded. "What are you waiting for?"

An instant later she was facedown over the kitchen table, her skirt at her hips, her sweet, round ass beckoning him. He couldn't get his pants off fast enough, could barely manage to slide on another condom.

He drove into her with an apology on his lips. He'd never started to come this fast, didn't know what was wrong with him. But she was writhing and crying out beneath him, and as he pushed down the top of her dress to cup and squeeze her breasts, he realized she was coming, too.

Melissa was any man's wet dream.

CHAPTER NINETEEN

Dominic left early the next morning for an appointment with the Outlaws' physical therapist and she decided to head into the office to watch JP's game tapes and take notes.

Which was when she realized exactly how screwed she really was.

She'd always had a good instinct for players—even her father thought so, which was high praise—but not this time. Although JP had all the right moves, they just didn't come together into a cohesive package. Obviously he'd gotten into the pros because he was a natural athlete. But making it in the pros took a whole lot more than innate talent.

Had her father ever dealt with a situation like this? She didn't think so—but she couldn't exactly ask him. Not when she'd made a point of being able to handle everything on her own.

Maybe she'd ask Dominic tonight. He'd promised to make her dinner, and sworn that they'd actually eat it this time.

Suddenly the door was flung open.

"Have you seen this yet?" her father asked in a hard voice as he waved a newspaper clipping in the air.

She frowned. "I don't know. Let me see it."

He wadded the paper into a ball and threw it at her. It was the most unprofessional thing she'd ever seen him do. Holding on to the tenuous thread of her pride, she fished it out from beneath a row of chairs and smoothed it out. Her father flicked the light on and she blinked in horror.

Last night at a benefit for the San Francisco Aquarium, unrestricted free agent JP Jesse told us that his new agent is "one hot babe." Which begs the question: Exactly how close is the lovely agent with her new client?

Angered by her father's low opinion of her taste in men, she said coldly, "JP is my client. That's all. I'll talk to him about watching his mouth."

"I don't want to see something like this in the press about one of my agents ever again. Understood?"

"Understood."

Her father was right, and she'd been skating on thin ice with Dominic for too long. She had to decide between being with Dominic and being his agent. Given that Dominic didn't want to be her "real" boyfriend, the choice was easy. Now she just had to tell him that they were through.

A few hours later, she knocked on Dominic's front door. Opening it, he kissed her as if he were dying of thirst and she was water. Following him into the kitchen, her heart in her throat due to what she had to say, she noticed that he had a faint limp. One of the hardest-working guys on the Outlaws, Dominic pushed himself every day, both on-season and off.

"How was practice today?"

He pulled ingredients out of his stainless steel Sub-Zero refrigerator. "A bitch. Like always." He grinned. "You want to know what got me through?"

She had a sinking feeling that whatever he said was only going to make it harder for her to break things off.

He pulled her against him. "Thinking about the next time I take you, someplace you aren't expecting to make love. The way you're going to have to swallow your moans of pleasure so no one in the next room hears how hard you're coming."

She swallowed hard. Just as he leaned in to kiss her, she said, "I watched JP's game tapes today."

Dominic stiffened and released her. She hated how cold she felt without his heat.

"What'd you think?"

"I'm not—"

Her purse started vibrating on the counter. She unzipped it and reached for her cell phone, checking the caller ID.

"It's JP." She was pleased at how furiously Dominic started to chop the celery as she clicked her phone open.

"Ms. McKnight?"

She rolled her eyes. At least he wasn't calling her babe anymore.

"You're not on a hot date tonight, are you?"

She glanced up at the gorgeous man standing five feet away, busily preparing a gourmet dinner for her. She most certainly was.

"No, I'm not."

"Good," JP said, sounding like a little kid who'd just been given his favorite treat. "I need your help with a very important decision."

"What is it?" With a guy like JP, it could be which shirt to wear.

"I'll tell you when you get here," he said.

The signal went dead and she held her phone away from her ear and stared at it.

"What's the little punk need now?" Dominic asked.

She shook her head. "I don't know. But evidently it's urgent."

Dominic looked her in the eye. "Don't go."

More than anything, she wanted to stay here with Dominic. But she couldn't do that. She had to tell him they were through. Done. Over.

Yet she couldn't spit it out yet; everything in her heart rebelled against it. She'd tell him soon.

"I have to go."

"Stay," he urged, moving toward her.

But if she let him touch her, she'd never be able to get away. And once she was naked in his bed, she'd never be able to tell him to get lost. Soon someone in the business would find out about them and share their dirty little secret with the world. JP would demand a new agent because he was pissed at her for not showing up, and it all added up to one thing: nothing. If he touched her, she'd be left with nothing. No hot sex and no clients.

"He's my client. He needs me."

Dominic snarled. "He needs a babysitter."

"Then that's what I need to be." She threw the door open and practically ran down the hall to the elevator, and pressed the red button over and over. She really needed to stop leaving Dominic's condo like this.

*

When Melissa got out of the cab at JP's house, she was surprised to see several cars parked in his huge driveway. Suddenly she wondered if she was being played.

JP's front door was partially open and she walked in without knocking. Several very thin girls with fake breasts and tight, skimpy clothes were lounging in the living room, and they glanced at her dismissively. Melissa pulled her shoulders back. She was proud of her curves. Apart from sheer genetics, she enjoyed food too much to ever look like these women.

JP appeared at the top of the stairs. "My number-one woman is finally here!"

This was why she never dated guys her own age; they were so immature.

"Come upstairs," he said.

"Do you need us, too?" one of the other women asked in a breathy voice.

JP grinned at his harem. "Why don't you girls play a little strip Twister while you wait for me?"

Melissa nearly burst out laughing when the girls actually started rooting through JP's things for the game.

She followed JP down the hall to his bedroom.

"I had that bed specially made," he boasted.

"Great." Fatigue washed through her. It had been a long week. "What do you need, JP?"

He led her into an enormous walk-in closet. "I want a big endorsement this year."

She nodded. "I'm going to get you one. As soon as we find a team." A player like Dominic was an easy sell to advertisers. He was a good-looking guy who consistently won games and stole women's hearts. JP, for all his talent, might be a mere flash in the pan. Advertisers weren't willing to shell out the big bucks on a guy who might not be playing next season.

"Since I'm here, you and I might as well have a little talk."

JP flipped through a dozen identical black shirts. "Whatever you have to say is what I want to hear."

She said firmly, "JP, you need to get serious about your playing, about the reality of your prospects."

He shot her a glance. "I thought that was your job."

She nodded. "It is, but you need to help me out by keeping your mouth shut." She handed him the newspaper clipping. "I'm not your 'babe.' I'm your agent."

He cocked his head. "But I meant this as a compliment."

"I appreciate that, JP," she said in a softer tone, "but it makes us both look bad."

He looked at her with respect. "I like that you're willing to come over here on a Friday night and tackle my ass. And actually, I was wondering about your friend."

"Alice?"

His face lit up. "I can't figure her out. And I like a woman I can barely keep up with."

Oh? Judging by the women downstairs, what JP really liked were women he could run mental circles around.

"You think she'd come out with me tonight?"

"No."

He looked at her like a puppy she'd just kicked. "Call her. Ask her."

"She's busy." Melissa lied to protect her friend.

His face fell. "If you say so." He started taking off his clothes.

"What are you doing?" she asked, taking a step backward.

"Going out. I need you to help me figure out what to wear."

"I'm afraid that's something you'll have to figure out yourself. I'll give you some privacy," she said, furious with him for dragging her over to his house for no reason.

As she left, he said, "I want you to come out with me tonight so we can get to know each other."

"Okay." He'd readily accepted her criticism, and now it was her turn to give a little. Even though she had a sixth sense that nothing good could come of this outing.

As she waited in the living room with the giggly

groupies, she wondered if anything had happened between Alice and JP last night. Unable to find Alice at the aquarium, Melissa had taken a cab home from the party. And her friend hadn't answered her cell phone all day. Melissa desperately hoped Alice hadn't pinned any romantic dreams on JP: He was a player through and through.

Alice and JP would never work. Just like she and Dominic never would, either.

CHAPTER TWENTY

Dominic couldn't remember the last time a woman had walked out on him. When he wanted a woman, he got her. Even as the years went by, he'd never felt threatened by the younger players, on the field or off. If a woman wanted to be with some young hotshot she could twist around her finger with a sexy glance, Dominic wasn't interested.

Melissa had never been that kind of girl. As far as he knew, she'd never dated an athlete, and certainly not one of her father's players. And she didn't sleep around.

Just the thought of another guy seeing her naked made Dominic see red.

She was his.

He threw their dinner into the trash. JP had called only to fuck with her. Didn't she realize that? He didn't need business advice; he just wanted to get under her skirt.

Dominic yanked a paper towel off the roll so hard that the stainless steel holder broke away from the wall. He had to save her. Had to bring her back where she belonged: with him.

Dominic grabbed his keys and headed for the garage. It didn't matter what her father was going to say; it didn't matter than his practices had gone from okay to crap after two sleepless nights of loving her. It didn't even matter that he did risky-ass things when he was with her, that he was powerless to stop himself from having sex in locker rooms and empty buildings and construction sites.

She was his.

And he refused to let her go.

Guys like JP were religious about their Friday-night partying. Whatever that punk needed from Melissa wouldn't take longer than an hour—which gave Dominic time to buy her flowers.

There hadn't been a lot of wooing yet, and he wanted to change that. He wanted her to know that he cared about her beyond their explosive sexual connection. He wanted her to know that she was unlike any woman he'd ever known. Melissa was soft and warm, yet filled with an inner strength that he wasn't certain she fully recognized.

All at once, he could see her with their children— a big crew of boys and girls with her wide laugh and expressive eyes. She'd been right there in front of his eyes for so many years—how had he managed to miss her?

A middle-aged woman was just turning the Closed sign face out on the flower-store door when Dominic double parked his car in front. She shook her head as if to say "sorry."

Dominic put his hands together in front of his chest, giving her a charming grin and a persuasive glint of his eyes.

She shook her head and laughed, then opened the door. "Come in," she said in a lilting Irish accent.

"Thank you," he said, full of gratitude at her kindness.

She chuckled. "Just so you know, I'm not doing this for you because you're a famous man who plays with balls."

"Whatever the reason, I really appreciate it."

She nodded. "My son watches your games every weekend. When he grows up, he wants to run around and get sweaty and dirty just like you." While she spoke, she pulled various flowers and greens out of plastic buckets. When she returned to her wooden worktop, she nimbly arranged the stunning bouquet. "You badly need these flowers, don't you?"

"I do," he admitted. "They're for a very special woman." It felt good to say the words aloud—not just to the woman but to himself, as well.

She turned her attention back to the thin purple ribbon she was tying around the stems. "I know she is. And that's why I decided to make you this bouquet." She handed it to him, waving away his credit card. "You have the eyes of a man very much in love."

The woman's statement knocked around inside Dominic. He felt like she was one step ahead of him. And that she was right.

"You must tell her," she said. "Tonight, when you give her these flowers."

Again, she was correct. He'd screwed up far too many times with Melissa. It was time to do something right.

"I will."

It had taken him thirty-six years to find his perfect mate, and he wasn't going to wait another day to make her his.

He parked in front of Melissa's apartment building, his heart pounding hard and fast. Women had always come so easily to him that he'd never had to put himself out on the line before.

Would she even consider loving him once he revealed the secret he'd hidden from everyone for so long?

He rang her doorbell. The seconds ticked by without a response. Had something happened to her? He pulled his cell phone out of his pocket. Her phone rang and rang, and he hung up when he got her voice mail. Something was wrong. He could feel it.

He sat down on the top step. He needed to calm down and think about the situation calmly. In all likelihood, JP was forcing her to sit in his living room and watch every game he'd ever played. The thought brought a lopsided smile to Dominic's face. He'd gotten the sense that she was none too impressed with JP's playing. And why would she be, since it was mostly showboating?

He was just standing up when a Hummer limo rounded the corner, loud rock music blasting from the open sun roofs. Dominic's mouth tightened. He wasn't surprised when the limo stopped in front of Melissa's apartment building and two barely dressed blondes stepped out. He also wasn't surprised that he wanted to wrap his hands around JP's neck, and that he didn't care whether the little pipsqueak lived.

JP hopped out onto the pavement, pulling Melissa along with him. "Well, well, well," JP smirked, looking damn pleased. "Who would've thought we'd find the great Dominic DiMarco hanging out in Noe Valley?"

Melissa's mouth was tight, her eyes wary. "What are you doing here, Dominic?" She looked at the flowers and her lips formed a small O. She dragged her gaze away from the bright arrangement and back at him. "I'm assisting JP tonight. You knew that."

JP snapped his fingers. "I've got a killer idea. Why don't you come out with us tonight, old man? You can show us your retro moves."

Melissa shot JP a killer glare. "Dominic is busy." She gestured to the flowers. "I'm sure he has a date tonight."

Didn't she realize they were on the verge of something really special? He needed to keep an eye on JP—and any other guy who tried to move in on his territory. Once he got her alone, he'd say those three important words.

"A night out sounds good," he agreed.

Melissa stomped up the stairs and pushed him aside to unlock the front door. "I don't want you to go," she hissed.

"Why not?" He enjoyed the way the tiny hairs on her arm stood up when he put his hand on the small of her back to guide her inside. "Are you afraid we'll do something crazy tonight in front of everyone? In front of JP?"

JP followed with his arms around the two groupies. "I bet you girls are excited about meeting another Outlaw, huh?"

One of the girls stared blatantly at Dominic's crotch. "I certainly am."

"Hey, Dom," JP said, "meet Jilly and Judy. They always come as a pair."

JP's pun wasn't exactly a shocker. Dominic had

met dozens of women over the years who got into athletes' beds by promising a hot threesome. Some guys even bragged about scoring with three or four women at a time. But that had never been Dominic's style. When he was with a woman he gave her his complete attention.

He held up his hand. "Nice to meet you," he said, as they went down the hall to Melissa's apartment. Yet again, he noted her warm, colorful style.

"If I'd known you all were going to come over," she muttered, "I would have cleaned."

A small stack of dishes sat in the sink and a sweater lay over the arm of the couch, but her apartment wasn't messy. It was lived in. It was just the way he wanted his condo to look—with Melissa's shoes kicked off by the front door, her mail on the kitchen counter, her keys tossed into a bowl on the entry table.

JP and his girls headed for her bedroom without asking permission.

"I'm going to teach him a lesson about manners," Dominic growled.

Melissa put her hand on his arm. "Don't," she said. "He doesn't mean any harm."

Dominic moved closer to her, backing her up against the front door. "You're wrong," he warned, his mouth close to hers. "He does."

JP called out from down the hall, "Where do you

keep your sexy clothes? We can't find any in this closet."

She shoved Dominic away, her cheeks flushed. "JP's my client. I'm getting to know him." Her eyes flashed a challenge. "I need him, Dominic. You know I do. Don't screw this up for me."

Dominic watched her head down to her bedroom. Somehow, he was going to have to keep his hands off her tonight.

And his fists off JP's face.

CHAPTER TWENTY-ONE

S itting in the hottest club in the city, surrounded
by beautiful women and hot men, Melissa felt
utterly out of her element.

JP had a girl on each thigh, both trying desperately
to win his attention. Melissa felt sorry for the groupies. Didn't they see that the more they vied for JP's
attention, the less they got of it?

"Hey, Dom," JP said, "aren't you thirsty?"

While everyone else at the table was putting back
bubbly like it was a dollar a bottle rather than a hundred, Dominic stuck with sparkling water.

"I'd rather win than drink," was his short reply.

Melissa hid her grin. It wouldn't do for JP to think
she was taking sides, but he could learn a thing or two
from Dominic.

The groupies had tried to cling to Dominic like
Saran Wrap, but he was a forbidding, big, dark pack-

age when he wanted to be. And he was downright scary tonight. Any playfulness had been replaced by fierceness.

And damn if it didn't turn her on like crazy.

JP grinned at Melissa. "Having fun?"

She nodded. "This is great. Lots of fun." For added impact, she took a sip of her champagne. She envisioned years of accompanying JP on the party circuit, and shuddered with distaste. Not exactly what she had in mind when she'd gotten her MBA. Maybe she could hire a cute, young assistant to take over this aspect of the job. She'd rather be on her couch under a blanket in front of the TV.

The music in the club changed from quick and driving to slow and sensual. Her pulse thrummed beneath her skin, and Dominic's eyes moved to her throat.

She stared into her fizzing champagne, unable to fight the fantasy of Dominic asking her to dance. Then someone was taking her hands in his, but although the hands were big and strong, they belonged to the wrong man.

JP pulled her up out of her chair. "Show me what you've got."

"No. This is a bad idea," she said.

"I get it if you're scared."

A challenge lay behind JP's words, and she knew that he was asking if she was tough enough to represent him.

She was.

Melissa raised one eyebrow. "You're the one everyone's going to be watching out there," she countered. "So you'd better bring your A game."

He threw his head back and laughed. "You look like a pussycat," he said, "but you act like a tiger." JP shot a loaded look at Dominic. "Watch closely, old man, and you just might learn something."

When JP pulled her close against his body, Melissa was so shocked she lost her words.

"You're not like those other girls," he murmured in what she assumed was supposed to be his sexy voice.

She forced a smile at his compliment and put a couple more inches of air between them.

"You're smart *and* sexy," he added.

"I'm also your agent. We need to talk about professional boundaries."

"Don't talk," he interrupted her. "Just feel."

She *wasn't* feeling it, and she didn't think he was, either. This was just part of his "I'm so bad" act.

"I have to pee," she said loudly into his ear.

JP jumped back several inches. "Damn, you sure know how to ruin a moment."

She turned and headed toward what she hoped were the bathrooms. Pushing aside a thick red velvet curtain, she found a perfect hiding spot.

But before she could get too comfortable, her

skin began to buzz with awareness. What the hell? She reacted like this only around Dominic.

A moment too late, she realized that Dominic had followed her behind the red curtain.

And he looked every inch the warrior.

Like a man who would die in battle for his woman in a heartbeat.

✳

"Dominic," Melissa said in a breathy voice that spoke straight to his cock.

He advanced on her, backing her into the wall, and put one hand on either side of her face.

"We're leaving," he said. "Now."

He knew better than to boss a woman around, especially a strong-willed woman like Melissa. But he couldn't control his mouth any more than he could control his body.

She stared at him without blinking. "No."

His mouth tightened, his gaze dropping to her full, red lips. "You have two choices," he said in a low voice, not taking his eyes from her mouth.

Her tongue shot into the sweet corner where her lips came together. "I'll do what I want," she whispered.

Sweet lord, her words sounded like a come-on. He knew they couldn't be, not when he was being an overbearing, horny prick—but his cock didn't care, growing to an impossible size beneath his zipper.

"Choice one," he said, "we leave this minute and I take you home. Choice two: I take you right here, right now, like this. Against the wall in the back of the club."

Her breath came out in a whoosh.

What Dominic read in her face was that she wanted him as much as he wanted her.

"You wouldn't dare," she challenged, her words raw with need.

He leaned in close, his mouth less than an inch from her ear. "Choice two it is." Then his mouth was on hers, his hands pulling up her dress.

But even in the insanity of his desire, no matter how much her body sang its need for his touch, he needed her to agree before he took things further.

He pulled back just enough to look down into her flushed face. God, she was beautiful. The most beautiful woman he'd ever seen. The words *I love you* rushed to the tip of his tongue, but he couldn't say them here. Not until they were alone.

"Say the word, and I'll leave you alone."

His heart pounded hard as he waited for her decision. He wouldn't use *I love you* to get her to agree to have sex with him in public.

"I can't," she said in a harsh whisper. "I can't let you go."

He didn't need to hear anything else. Her mouth tasted like sugar and grapes as their tongues tangled together. Their previous lovemaking had been extraordinary, but now ecstasy warred with violence as her hands pulled and scraped at his clothes, ripping the inside seams of his jacket, her fingernails scratching his skin as she pulled him harder against her body.

Dominic knew his own strength and held on to it tightly at all times—in both anger and passion—but when Melissa's teeth nipped at his mouth, his jaw, his neck, he lost his grip.

In a millisecond her ass was in his hands and her skirt was up around her hips. Their pelvises ground hard against each other's and he felt her oncoming orgasm a moment before she did, working his finger between their bodies, rubbing it over her clit, the slick folds of her pussy, and then all the way inside her as her muscles clenched and pulled at him.

He had to get in there, *now*. Seconds later, his pants were unzipped and a condom was on and his shaft was pressing into her heat. She moaned his name and it sounded almost like a curse as he pushed high and hard into her, stretching her wide. She smelled like sex and she tasted like sex, and it wouldn't have mattered if someone had walked in just then—he wouldn't have been able to stop fucking her.

She held on to his neck, and with her legs wrapped tightly around his waist, he moved his hands from her sweet, round ass to cup her face. She rode him hard, using her strong thigh muscles to plunge up and down on his cock. Her skin grew damp with exertion, and he roared his pleasure into her mouth, his cock throbbing and pulsing into her heat.

With surprising strength, she pushed away from his body and rapidly adjusted her clothes, her eyes cast down. She was shutting him out.

"Did I hurt you?" he asked, hating the thought of harming her in anyway.

"No. I'm fine. Everything's fine. I need to get back out there. JP is going to wonder what happened to us."

And although Dominic was famed for his lightning-quick reactions on the field, he stood still as a stone as he watched her walk back through the red curtain.

CHAPTER TWENTY-TWO

Melissa blinked into the neon lights surrounding the dance floor as she emerged from the darkness. She didn't know how long she'd been gone, how long she'd been riding Dominic's huge cock, but in those minutes everything had changed.

She had changed.

She'd never thought of herself as ballsy, but she'd assumed at least she knew her own mind. She'd thought she was strong enough to risk a dangerous desire, but she was wrong. She was incapable of resisting Dominic.

She was so damn angry! Angry at herself for being weak, angry with Dominic for making her want so much more than she could have, for showing her possibilities no other man could ever live up to.

JP crooked a finger at her from the dance floor while gyrating his hips seductively. Feeling Dominic emerge behind her, she allowed her hips to sway back and forth in rhythm to the music. She wanted to lose herself in the music, in the darkness, in the strangers all around her.

She moved to join JP on the dance floor and let him pull her against him. She was safe with him. As long as JP was by her side, Dominic couldn't overtake her soul with his sensuality.

Sure, he demanded, but *she* was the one who delivered, who couldn't say no.

Her skin grew damp as she danced. She was exhausted from too little sleep and too much sex, but there was safety in numbers on the dance floor.

Finally, JP whispered in her ear, "It's time to go home now."

She shook her head. "No."

Going home meant time to think about Dominic. Time to admit how weak she was.

"They're locking up and kicking us out," JP said as he pushed her toward the door. "Warrior man over there has been glaring at us for the past four hours."

Dominic was standing by the front door with his muscular arms crossed over his chest.

As the distance closed between her and Dominic, she moved closer to JP to stay away from temptation.

Dominic's face was a dark cloud, his eyes black with fury.

She deliberately smiled at JP. "Thank you for an incredible night."

Dominic had always been a calm, solid presence on a team full of unpredictable men. But now he looked anything but: his fists were tight, his jaw locked, his eyes narrowed.

She didn't care. *Now it's your turn. I hope you're jealous.* It was the only power she had over him.

As the blocks ticked away and they drew closer to her apartment, her breathing grew shallow.

She needed to find a subtle way to convince JP to guard her until Dominic got out of the limo and drove away in his Viper. The limo stopped and she said, "JP, I just remembered that we need to discuss a couple of important issues tonight. Do you have a few minutes?"

Dominic remained in his seat in the limo, obviously intent on waiting for her to finish her "business" with JP. No matter how long it took. Or how lame it was.

JP stretched and yawned, his arms ending up around the girls cuddled against him. "I'm too tired. Let's talk tomorrow."

Damn it, he clearly didn't have her back. But then it wasn't his job to protect her from Dominic, who had just stepped out of the limo and was holding the door open for her to make her way past JP's girls. As she stepped out onto the sidewalk, Dominic closed the limo door with an ominous click and it sped away.

"We need to talk," he said in a hard voice.

"Fine," she said, her response clipped and edgy as she rummaged through her bag for her keys.

He followed her silently up the stairs and down the long hall to her door. As she hung her keys on the hook in her foyer, Dominic closed the door behind him.

"Are you thinking straight? What the *hell* were you doing out there tonight?"

She went on the offensive. "If you're referring to sleeping with you in every possible location through the city this week, no—I definitely am not thinking straight."

"I'm not talking about us," he said in a low, dangerous voice. "I'm talking about JP. Don't you realize you're ruining your career before it even begins? We all saw you and JP out there tonight. The way you were letting him touch you."

Melissa couldn't believe what she was hearing. "We were only dancing together. He went to his harem for other fun."

"No—he wants you. They all do. Someone needs to warn you, before it's too late and you lose everything you've worked for."

Melissa pushed her finger into his hard chest. "I can't believe you actually have the nerve to warn me about JP's motives!" *He* was the one breaking all the rules, not JP.

"You're nothing to him," Dominic said. "Nothing more than just another fuck."

She felt so cold, as if her blood had all drained away, leaving ice in its wake.

"I get it," she said. "I can't believe it took me this long to get it." A harsh laugh escaped. "Don't worry, I don't want anything from you, Dominic. In fact, I was going to tell you tonight that we're through. Done."

"Shit, that came out all wrong. I'm not talking about *us*. Being with you has been much more than just a screw."

She laughed bitterly. "I don't believe you."

He was shaking his head, but she was sick and tired of his endless power over her. She put her hand on her doorknob and yanked it open. "Get out."

He remained standing in her foyer. "I love you."

She hated him then, hated him for pulling the one card out of his deck that could break her. "No, you don't. If you loved me, you wouldn't have come into my house and said those horrible things."

Remorse filled his face. "I do love you, Melissa."

"Leave me *alone*."

An eternity passed, then she watched him walk out of her apartment, out of her life.

Before he went down the hall, he stopped and spoke. "You are my true soul mate, Melissa."

Her tears dropped onto the floor; she wanted to cover her ears and block him out. Couldn't he see that he wasn't being fair?

"One day you'll see it. And when you do, I'll be waiting."

He closed the door and was gone.

She slid to the floor. Wrapping her arms around her knees, she rocked back and forth as sobs twisted her inside out.

CHAPTER TWENTY-THREE

During a game, when Dominic screwed up, he didn't waste anyone's time apologizing; he just made it clear to his teammates and coach that he'd make the necessary changes to get the next play right. Making a mistake was human. Making it again was pathetic—and unforgivable.

After fifteen years, he had it all figured out on the football field. But he was an idiotic fuck-up when it came to Melissa. One image after another assaulted him as he got into his car.

Melissa sitting on the bar stool at Barnum's, tipsy and sexy.

Losing control in his living room and taking her incredible naked body up against the window.

The way her face fell the next morning when he told her it was just an aberration.

In Jason's restaurant, where she blew his mind again, with an incredible morning following closely.

The clanging of metal in the locker room as he thrust against her.

The policeman knocking on his fogged-up window after one of the most explosive sexual experiences of his life.

The hatred on her face as he accused her of acting like a whore with JP.

Dominic had never felt like such an asshole. Driving as if on autopilot, he blindly made his way home. He stepped into his condo and it felt cold. Empty. Sure, he was a rich, famous, good-looking man. But without Melissa, his life would be nothing more than a string of empty one-night stands with women who couldn't hold a candle to the one he loved with all his heart.

Somehow, someway, he needed to figure out a way to make it up to her. To convince her that he really and truly loved her, and would never behave so poorly again. Winning Melissa back was all that mattered now.

And unfortunately, he needed JP to get back into her heart.

*

When Melissa finally fell asleep that night, she dreamed she was living in a castle under attack by marauding bands of outlaws and Dominic was an avenging warrior, willing to give up his life to save hers. As he plunged his sword into the final outlaw, then swept her up into his arms, his lips so close to hers that she could already taste him, she woke up.

It was no use. How could she sleep when he'd finally said the three words she'd longed to hear all her life: *I love you?* *And* used those words as a weapon, to get her to forgive the horrible things he'd said and agree to fuck him some more.

Today she had to join the McKnight clients on the practice field for the Outlaws' annual summer scrimmage. It was her job to keep an eye on the players during the off season, to note who looked tired, who needed more rest, who should put in more hours at the gym to build up his strength.

She used to wait all year long for this because it was her one chance to stare at Dominic openly, fantasizing about being with him. Now she questioned everything.

Had she been too easy on him? Had she been so infatuated with the image he presented that she hadn't wanted to see the real man beneath?

Guys like JP and Ty Calhoun didn't hide their arrogance, their womanizing. On the contrary, they almost seemed proud of their flaws.

Suddenly it seemed like Dominic had tried too hard to be the perfect guy.

She took a cab to the practice field, dreading

every second to come. Somehow, she needed to keep her shit together when Dominic ran out onto the field.

"Melissa," JP called out as she walked onto the grass. "Thanks for hooking me up with this gig. It'll be good to play a little, show everyone my stuff."

How did he look so fresh, so energetic?

She tried to return his grin and failed.

He moved closer, his expression growing unchar-acteristically serious.

"You don't look so good. Something happen last night after I dropped you off?" He looked over his shoulder at the players stretching on the field. "Did dirty Dom finally make a move?"

She shook her head. "Of course not. I just slept poorly. It's been a long time since I danced like that. I'm pretty sore."

Turning back into the JP she expected, he looked her up and down appreciatively. "If you need a rub-down, let me know." He held up his hands. "These babies are magic."

She managed a real smile. Who'd have thought she'd actually like him? He was a fuck-up, but at his core he was a nice guy. To a girl like her, who just wasn't attracted to him, he was harmless.

"I'll have to take your word for it," she said, know-ing it was her job to build up his ego. "I'll be taking notes on your performance today, then we'll sit down and discuss everything Monday morning. How you play today means a lot. Don't blow it."

JP picked up a football. "All of a sudden you're reminding me of my ninth-grade math teacher." He whistled. "She was tough. And hot."

Melissa had to laugh as he ran onto the field. If she could figure out a way to channel JP's erotic humor into a mainstream market, they'd be turning away endorsement offers in droves.

Melissa's father called out her name and she headed to the shaded seating area on the sidelines.

"Good morning," she said coolly when she reached his side, still angry with him for the way he'd talked to her yesterday.

"I thought I made myself perfectly clear yesterday," he said in a hard voice.

Her heart plunged into her shoes. Shit. He knew about last night. On the heels of the news clipping, no wonder he was angry.

"Word spreads fast in this business. I'd be careful whose invitation to go dancing you accept in the future."

"Melissa doesn't need to apologize for her behavior," Dominic's deep, sexy voice said behind her.

When had he crept up on them? Shooting a glance at her father, she noted the red splotches staining his cheeks.

"You should be praising Melissa for the excellent job she did of entertaining her two clients last night," Dominic said.

Tom's eyebrows drew together. "You were there, too? I thought JP and Melissa had . . ."

How could her father possibly think she'd fall for a slick horndog like JP? She was way smarter than that.

And if Dominic hadn't barged into their conversation, "rescuing" her, she'd have had the satisfaction of giving her father a piece of her mind. Instead, he'd swiped it right out from under her.

And that's when it hit her: Dominic and her father were two of a kind. Neither of them trusted her to make the right decisions. Neither of them thought she was capable of taking care of herself.

She held up her hand. *"Enough.* I've heard more than enough. I'm here this morning to take notes on how my clients are playing." She gave Dominic a hard look. "They're waiting for you on the field."

His dark eyes were unreadable. With a curt nod he headed onto the field, his helmet gripped tightly in his hand.

Then she met her father's eyes. "Here's the deal. For one week, you aren't going to second-guess me. You aren't going to lecture me. And you aren't going to jump to conclusions. I'm going to work with my clients however I see fit. If JP hasn't signed with a new team by the end of the week

and you deem my performance unworthy of the McKnight Agency, you can fire me. No hurt feelings. No recriminations."

A muscle in her father's jaw jumped in anger. "I'm trying to figure out why I shouldn't just fire you right now. If any other agent spoke like this to me, he'd be history."

Melissa shrugged. "You certainly could do that." She wasn't afraid of her father anymore, and wondered why she ever had been. "But then, you might risk losing your best agent."

He blinked once. Twice. "One week," he said, then walked to the group of agents over by the doughnuts and coffee.

Melissa's mouth curved into a smile. She'd finally surprised him. For the first time in his life, it seemed he didn't recognize the woman standing before him. Maybe he'd never really known her at all.

And maybe she hadn't known herself.

She took a seat and tried to focus on JP's blocking and pass routes, but she was continually distracted by Dominic.

Though not for the usual reasons.

Dominic had always been one of the most consistently excellent players in football. Where most guys had their share of down games—even a down season, if things were really rotten—Dominic earned his salary every single outing. His plays were inspired, finessed, and rarely outmaneuvered by the defensive line.

But this morning he was a bona fide disaster, with a bad case of the drops. He couldn't hold on to anything thrown his way. She winced as he was crushed beneath a linebacker. She'd have been embarrassed for him if she hadn't been so worried about the pain he had to be in.

Her father's words came back to her: *He's getting close to retirement.*

After one bad play too many, Dominic limped over to the sidelines and JP moved in to replace him. Come Monday morning, no matter how much pain Dominic was in, as his agent she'd have to lay down some hard truths. If he continued to perform so far below his usual level—especially if he took this crappy performance into the start of the new season—future endorsements, not to mention lucrative new contracts, would be very hard to come by.

But under no circumstances would she run to his side to make sure he was okay. Because that was something a girlfriend—or a wife—did.

Not a three-day fuck buddy like her.

The Outlaws' physical therapist pushed and flexed Dominic's arms and legs and chest. "Anything hurt?"

Dominic grunted. Everything did, just like always.

But although his body had taken a real beating on the field today, it was his pride that hurt like hell. He'd been asleep out there, a total liability.

Seeing Melissa look so pale and so sad had shaken him deeply. He'd never meant to cause her such pain. When she'd walked into the stadium that morning, he'd been struck again by the fact that she was the most beautiful woman he'd ever known. But his reaction was more than sexual. Her beauty went deeper than her face, her skin, her body.

She radiated goodness from within.

And she didn't trust him, didn't believe that he loved her.

And why the hell should she? he wondered as the therapist pulled his foot into his glutes to stretch his quads. He'd rejected her, seduced her, then lost his mind in her foyer and acted like a complete ass.

Dominic grunted at the painful stretch. Post-scrimmage had always been a time for reflection, but his thoughts usually centered on the game.

Today, the only thing he could focus on was Melissa.

"I've never seen you so tight," the therapist said. "Been doing anything out of the ordinary lately?"

Oh, just nonstop sex and guilt-induced insomnia.

"A couple of late nights," he finally said.

Matt began to work his torture on Dominic's other leg. "You sure are lucky," he said enviously.

"Regular guys like me have to work our asses off just to get a pretty girl's attention. You must have to turn them away like crazy."

Matt was right. The easy part was getting a girl into bed. The hard part was knowing when you had the right girl.

And making sure you didn't screw it up.

Fucking up in high school had made him shut down the wildness inside, allowing it to be unleashed only on the field. Had he turned into an emotionless scrooge? A man who couldn't recognize love when it slapped him in the face?

It had taken Melissa only three days to uncover a part of Dominic that he'd kept hidden nearly his whole life, to realize that his childhood had been all about responsibility. Without his telling her anything about his shithead stepfather, and the crushing guilt he'd lived with for two decades, somehow Melissa had tapped directly into Dominic's deep, dark core.

He'd always thought that passion was a weakness and had never allowed himself to feel this way about anyone else. But with Melissa, he'd had no choice.

He loved her. Passionately.

Somehow he needed to make up for the callous way he'd treated her. He needed to tell her he loved her again—the right way, without jealousy and possession clouding every word. He was going to admit all his sins.

And then, for once he'd sit the fuck back and listen to what she wanted, rather than what he thought was best for both of them.

He sat upon the massage table and flipped open his cell phone, then made the Hail Mary phone call that was his last chance to win Melissa back.

CHAPTER TWENTY-FOUR

Monday morning, Melissa walked into the conference room and locked the door. She was still recovering from the barbecue at her parents' house on Sunday. All afternoon, they'd pressed single men on her. Boring, balding, conceited men of all shapes and sizes brought her glasses of wine and told her how pretty she was. But mostly they admired her father's top-of-the-line outdoor grill and kitchen, knowing that if they married her, one day it would all be theirs. She couldn't wait to leave.

The telephone in the center of the conference table stared at her, daring her to call JP and tell him he was nowhere near ready to play for a new team. Because after seeing him play on Saturday, she'd known with utter certainty that she couldn't shop him yet—if ever.

JP was a train wreck: fast when he should have been

taking his time, catching the football either a moment too early or a millisecond too late. He had a great physique, but it didn't take much to get him panting.

Sure, she could run him until he dropped, make him start the day with weights and end it doing push-ups and sit-ups until he cried out for mercy. But it was more than conditioning that JP lacked. And frankly, Melissa wasn't at all sure that he had that special something.

The special something that Dominic had in spades.

She shouldn't think about him—it was pointless. She'd always love him beyond words, but she couldn't be with a man who wanted to control her.

Forcing herself to focus, Melissa picked up the phone and dialed JP's house. He wasn't home and didn't answer his cell phone either.

Great. Instead of working his ass off to become the best damn wide receiver in the country, he was probably out spending all the money he didn't have in expectation of a multimillion-dollar deal.

If JP hadn't been her only real client, she'd have fired him so fast his head would have spun.

The rest of the day, she made calls and sent emails to all the wide receivers the agency had ever worked with. She asked them what they thought set a great wide receiver apart from a good one, and the information they gave her was golden.

JP needed to run precise routes, have breakaway speed, and make catches even when he was double teamed. By the end of the day, Melissa had a plan for success. Now all she needed to do was find JP. And shove her plan down his pretty throat.

She had less than one week to transform JP from a crap client to solid gold. Four and a half short days to work a miracle. If she pulled this off, her father would have to kiss her feet.

Although suddenly her father's opinion didn't matter nearly as much as it used to.

The phone rang, and when she picked up, Angie got straight to the point: "Your father needs to see you. Now."

Hadn't she told her father to leave her the hell alone for the next week?

"Fine," she said, ready to give her father a piece of her mind.

Her father pushed back in his seat when she walked in. "I've got some strange news. Bad news."

Her heart thumped. "Mom?"

"No. Your mother is fine. It's about Dominic."

She paused, her heart in her throat, trying to brace herself for her father's revelations. "What? What is it?"

"I just got a call from my friend at *Sports Illustrated*. One of their writers was doing a piece on the greatest heroes in football, and Dominic's name was on the list." Her father rubbed his hand over his face. "Evidently the writer unearthed some dirt on Dominic. Something from his past."

Dominic had been hiding something from her? From all of them? Her heart ached for him, even as she worked to bury her hurt at not being confided in.

"Did your friend say what it was?"

"No. And given that Dominic's on the verge of retirement, this is the time for him to be thinking about autobiographies, speaking tours, and motivational visits to high-school auditoriums. We all stand to lose big here, but Dominic most of all. You need to find out what the hell he's been hiding, and fast. Then fix it even faster."

*

Sweat dripped into Dominic's eyes and he pushed it away with the back of his hand. For the past forty-eight hours at seven thousand feet in Lake Tahoe, where the air was a hell of a lot thinner than it was at sea level in San Francisco, he'd pushed his body to the limit.

But he'd pushed JP harder.

JP was squatting on the grass, bent over his knees, dry-heaving. He'd thrown up everything in his system by noon. By late afternoon he was sniveling.

Though to be fair, JP hadn't cried uncle yet. He couldn't—not if he wanted to keep his pride intact.

Dominic grinned. Training JP had been a hell of a lot more fun than he'd expected. He was getting great pleasure from watching JP suffer.

Dominic stood over him, blocking the sunlight. "Let's hit the weight room."

JP groaned. "Leave me the fuck alone."

"No can do, punk. Not until you stop sucking."

"Fuck you."

"If you can still talk, I must not be working you hard enough."

JP pulled himself up with the help of a nearby tree trunk. "One day I'll pay you back for this."

"I have no doubt you will. I'll give you a head start to the weight room."

JP glared at him. "Don't do me any favors."

Dominic shrugged, intent on pushing JP until he showed some goddamn backbone. "Three, two, one."

They shot off down the dirt road toward Dominic's Lake Tahoe house at breakneck speed. For the first time, Dominic had to push himself, rather than hold back so that JP didn't quit out of embarrassment.

Five minutes later, JP's hand made contact with the redwood deck a length ahead of Dominic. Despite himself, Dominic was impressed.

When JP wanted to, he could kick it into overdrive. To be that fast after two exhausting days when

Dominic had kept him running from five in the morning until midnight—that was impressive.

JP collapsed in the dirt, gasping, "Thanks."

Dominic leaned against the redwood rail. "Tell it to the bench press," he said, both of them knowing it was code for "you're welcome."

Dominic hadn't told JP why he'd decided to work with him, but he was pretty sure the guy knew he was doing it for Melissa. She deserved great clients. And since he figured his time in the pros was coming to an end, he could pass on some of what he'd learned over the past fifteen years to a young guy like JP.

No matter how hard they had to work, Dominic refused to let JP fail. Not when it meant that Melissa failed, too.

CHAPTER TWENTY-FIVE

Melissa tried everything—the phone, email, even a visit to his condo—but Dominic had disappeared. It wasn't until another Outlaw walked past her cubicle and overheard her leaving Dominic yet another voice mail that she found out he'd gone to Lake Tahoe.

"That's right. I'd forgotten," she lied.

She hated the fact that she was utterly in the dark about both of her clients.

Furious, she took a cab to the nearest car-rental agency. She certainly hadn't planned on a four-hour drive into the mountains tonight, and she nursed her anger throughout the long trip, cursing both their arrogance and her stupid dream of working with self-obsessed football players.

The sun had set by the time she pulled into a long dirt driveway. Pine trees stood tall on both sides of her car. Even in the dark, the setting was inescapably beautiful.

Climbing out of the car, she shivered in her thin cotton top. Evenings at Lake Tahoe were chilly. Her eyes grew huge as she stood in front of Dominic's house. Not at all ostentatious, even in the moonlight it was the most beautiful cottage she'd ever set eyes on.

She could picture herself running out onto the beach, chasing after children with towels, while Dominic stood on the deck behind the grill, flipping hamburgers and hot dogs.

Her eyes blurred with sudden tears, and she forcibly shook the images away. When would she accept that happily-ever-after was never going to happen?

Ignoring the doorbell, she pounded on the door and braced herself for Dominic's beautiful face. Instead, JP greeted her.

"I was wondering when you'd get here," he drawled.

She wanted to kick him. "What are you doing here?"

JP moved into the kitchen, bypassing a wine rack to grab a Perrier. "Want one?"

She shook her head.

"Suit yourself," he said, twisting the cap off his water and bringing it to his mouth.

JP was drinking water? Not wine, or bourbon, or

something else that would impede his performance on the field?

He put the bottle down and wiped his hand across his mouth. "Damn, that really hit the spot." He stretched his hands above his head and yawned. "I'm beat."

Frustration bubbled up inside her. "What, from all that sunbathing you've been doing by the lake? I was going to break the news to you in a nicer way, but I can't be bothered anymore. So here's the deal. I watched your game tapes and I wasn't impressed."

JP simply nodded. "I hear you, boss."

Caught off guard, she said, "You do?"

"Dominic has been showing me things."

She blinked.

"My timing is off," JP admitted. "I've been slacking off during workouts. I need to get off the line quicker."

She stared at JP in shock. He'd just listed several issues she'd planned on taking up with him. Once again, Dominic had beaten her to the punch. He was her knight in shining armor, taking care of everything.

If only it didn't smack of an apology—just like the way he'd offered to be her client after their first night together.

A sliding glass door opened and Dominic walked in, carrying a load of firewood. Melissa's eyes widened and her mouth watered. He'd obviously been chopping wood—without his shirt on.

She tried to resummon her resentment, but it was difficult to be angry with a man who looked as good as Dominic. Maybe if he'd been wearing a shirt she would have been able to string two thoughts together, but right now, all she could see was his sweat-slick chest, his muscular shoulders, and his—

"Melissa, I'm glad you're here," he said.

She had to reach deep within herself to keep her knees from turning to mush. "Planning on mentioning this situation with JP to me anytime soon?"

He put down the wood and approached her, all effortless confidence. "Let me explain."

Didn't he realize she couldn't possibly have this conversation with him unless he was covered from head to toe—and wearing a bag over his head, too? Then again, maybe he knew *exactly* what he was doing. It probably wasn't the first time he'd used his looks to get something he wanted.

"Get dressed and then I'll talk to you." Turning her back on him, she faced JP, who'd been watching their dialogue with interest. "But you and I are going to talk right now."

She walked into the family room of the lakefront house, forcing down another vision of family and kids and laughter. From now on, she was 100 percent business.

JP lowered himself down onto a couch and put his bare feet up on the coffee table. "You guys need me to get out of here?"

Melissa frowned. "I'll speak with Dominic in private. After I'm done with you."

JP rubbed his chin. "I can't believe I'm about to do this."

"Then don't," she said, feeling the beginnings of a headache.

He laid his hand over his heart. "I just can't keep it in."

She rolled her eyes.

"Here's the thing, boss," he said. "I'm all about feeling the love. And I'm feeling it right now."

"Please don't." JP wasn't about to confess that he had feelings for her, was he? That would just be ugly.

"Don't worry," he said, chuckling. "I'm not in love with you." He looked her up and down. "Even if—and I mean this in the most respectful way—you are a supremely hot piece of ass."

"I think we're done with this conversation now, JP."

"I'm talking about you and Dom."

Her heart thudded. "We just work together."

JP smiled. "I still find it hard to believe you'd pick an old man like him over me."

She shook her head in denial. "I haven't picked him."

"Don't worry, he didn't tell me anything. Just a good guess. And seeing you guys together just now really made things clear."

What did JP see that she didn't? She wanted to grab him by the throat and shake the answers out of him.

Dominic walked into the room and JP shot up off the couch. "Gotta go meet some pretty Tahoe girls. See ya."

"Don't touch a drop of alcohol," Dominic warned.

"I've been listening, teach. I'm going to stay dry. Scout's honor."

Melissa desperately wished he would stay; she needed him as a buffer. Then the front door closed and she stared at Dominic, the silence stretching out between them.

He spoke first. "You've probably figured out why JP is here."

"You're training him."

"He's a fast learner."

"At least one of you is."

His expressive brown eyes widened with surprise.

"I get it," she said, "you're sorry. You want to make it up to me for the horrible things you said. Again."

His jaw tightened. "It's more than that."

She stood up. "Sure it is."

He took a step toward her. "I love you."

She forced out the sarcastic words: "Sure you do." She hated this but couldn't back down this time. Not ever again.

"I don't know what else to do to convince you."

She closed her eyes hard, then opened them and stared straight at him. "Just stop trying, okay? I'm your agent and you're my client, and that's all there ever was or ever will be between us."

Pain flashed across his face, but she couldn't let that stop her. "I came to give you some news," she said in a softer voice. "Bad news."

A flash of alarm crossed his face.

"A writer from *Sports Illustrated* has dug up some dirt from your past. I need to know what it is, Dominic. Anything and everything you can think of. We can turn this around, but we've got to do it quickly."

His eyes were bleak as he stared into the distance. "We can't turn this around. It's finally over."

She grabbed his hand and squeezed it hard. "What's over? What happened?"

His words came hard, fast. "I used to drink. Anything I could steal. From my mother's boyfriends, from my friends' parents. The liquor store's lock sucked. It was easy to break in and take what I wanted."

Melissa tried hard to conceal her surprise. "You were just a kid. People change."

"Stealing cars was even better. Me and my friend

Joe would hot-wire one, take it for a joyride, then leave it with an empty gas tank and a couple of smoked-up joints. Joe was heading to Virginia Tech on a football scholarship. We thought we were invincible. Then I drove into a tree."

A gasp escaped her before she could pull it inside. "You were okay?"

He nodded grimly. "I was fine. Joe wasn't. His legs were broken. He lost his scholarship."

It took everything she'd learned from watching her father to approach Dominic's revelations from a business perspective: This story could be a PR nightmare if it got out the wrong way. Still, her heart broke for the teenager Dominic had once been.

"How come I've never heard this story before?" she asked quietly. "How could something like this have been shoved under the rug for so long?"

"His parents were big into local politics. They couldn't let it get out that he was drinking and stealing cars."

"Dominic," she said softly, "you were just a kid. Kids do stupid stuff." His expression was bleak. "You've never forgiven yourself, have you?"

He didn't move, didn't blink. And then he shook his head. "No." His eyes begged her for forgiveness. "I wanted to tell you before now. I just didn't know how."

Stunned, she needed a few minutes to process everything.

"I've put my endorsements at risk," he said, obviously misreading her silence as worry and trying to manage the situation. "I don't care about the money; I don't need it. But now I've fucked up your career, too."

She held up her hand. "It's my job to worry about that. Not yours. We'll figure this out together."

His gaze cleared as he stared at her. "You'll stay?"

"I will." But she didn't trust herself to remain in his house. Not when she wanted to comfort him and the only way she knew how was with her body. "I'm going to spend the night in town. In the morning, we'll come up with a PR plan. And I'll help you train JP. I've got some ideas."

For the first time all night, Dominic smiled.

*

Dominic's body was so bruised and beaten that he fell asleep not long after Melissa left. But he woke up long before sunrise, haunted by everything Melissa had said.

She was right about him, about his actions being motivated by guilt. He loved her deeply, but working with JP was about assuaging his guilt.

He'd been doing the same thing for years with Joe. Houses, cars, boats—he bought them all, even when Joe said he didn't want them or need them.

Why the fuck had he railroaded his friend with

lavish gifts over the years? Joe was a smart guy, the CEO of his own company manufacturing "green" cleansers. He definitely didn't need Dominic's guilt offerings.

It was just as well that *Sports Illustrated* was going to out him. He should have owned up to his past a long time ago.

He got up, turned on the shower, and stood under the water.

It felt good to come clean.

CHAPTER TWENTY-SIX

The next morning passed in a blur of drills. Though Melissa was impressed by how hard JP was working, it would still be amazing if they pulled off a new deal. Especially with the cloud hanging over Dominic.

She'd finally accepted that things between her and Dominic would never work out. She'd built him up in her head for so many years, dreamed for so long about what he must be like, that she'd never been able to see him purely for himself. She hadn't been fair to him. Now she needed to find it in her heart to wish him well, to wish for him all the love and happiness that she wanted for herself.

"He's dragging," she said at lunchtime as they watched JP run laps around the nearby high-school track. She and Dominic were a surprisingly good team as they focused their energies on JP.

He agreed. "No point in killing the kid, I suppose." He whistled to get JP's attention. "Good work. Go get some lunch. We'll see you in an hour."

JP tried to smile but clearly couldn't muster the energy. "Ugh." He limped back to his car and drove back to the cottage, probably to sleep in the hot tub for an hour.

Melissa walked with Dominic back to his car. His Viper held so many memories for her. Every time she'd been in it they'd had sex before, during, or after their drive.

She shivered in response to the memories.

He pulled into a lakefront burger joint and Melissa was grateful that it wasn't romantic in the least. She hadn't eaten much in the last few days and her clothes were already getting loose. Knowing that the waif look didn't suit her, she ordered a bacon cheeseburger, fries, and a Coke.

They found a booth in the corner and sat down. Their food came, but neither of them ate.

Dominic spoke first. "I don't want to hide from my past."

Melissa's eyes widened in surprise. "I would never ask you to do that."

"I know you wouldn't. Other agents maybe, but not you."

Melissa took a deep breath. "I've been thinking things over all night long. I'm positive that we can turn your story into something positive, something that will hopefully make other teenage boys think twice before they steal a car and crash into a tree. You've already done so much by donating the high-school stadium."

"I can do more."

She nodded. "And you will. We will."

"Thank you for helping me. For listening and not being angry."

"Of course," she said, not knowing how to put her feelings into words.

"Now let me help you. Please."

Melissa's throat closed up. She'd been so afraid of letting Dominic take over, so scared that he wanted to help her for all the wrong reasons. But things were different now.

"Thank you, Dominic. I think I could have gotten JP a good team by working with him, but with your help, hopefully we can bring in a great team instead."

His body was tense, his hamburger untouched. "I'd like to set up a meeting for JP with Sean from the Outlaws."

She furrowed her brows in confusion. "The Outlaws already have enough wide receivers."

All at once, she understood. He was going to retire. She felt as if he'd punched her in the gut. She couldn't imagine the Outlaws without Dominic, a Sunday without him on the field. It was wrong. So wrong. Yet she knew he was hurting. She'd seen him limp, felt his scars beneath her fingertips.

He watched her process the news. "I've been thinking about it for a while now. I refuse to be a liability to my team, a disappointment to the fans."

It was difficult to speak. "How long have you been thinking about this?"

"It's been brewing for a while now, but working with JP really made things clear. I ran myself into the ground just to see if I could keep up with him."

"You can," she protested, still unwilling to accept his decision. It would be such a loss. "You're still a phenomenal player," she protested.

"I'm not healing like I used to. I wake up in the morning and I know the stiffness isn't going to be gone by the next day. I'm starting to dread blocking. That's not the kind of game I want to play."

"Okay," she said slowly, "we'll work out an exit plan." Emotionally, she hated the decision he was making. Professionally, she knew he was right.

"Obviously, you have a strong future ahead of you with speaking engagements, maybe some nonfiction, even fashion if you're interested." What the hell were the Outlaws going to do without the top wide receiver in the country? She hated having to break the news to the team.

He shook his head. "We'll see what happens once people find out about my past."

That pissed her off. "Dominic, you're an amazing man who made a mistake as a kid. Sure, maybe you should have come clean a long time ago, but your friend is doing fine now, isn't he?"

Somewhat reluctantly, Dominic nodded. "Better than fine. Great."

Her cell phone rang and she looked down at the small screen. "It's my father," she said, then clicked it open.

"I should have known you were sleeping with him."

Fear gripped her heart. "Excuse me?"

"I couldn't figure out why Dominic wanted to work with you," her father said. "Now I know."

"We're not—" she began, wanting desperately to deny her father's accusation. Even though it was true.

"Be in my office at eight a.m."

Tom severed their connection and Melissa carefully put the phone back down on the table next to her untouched burger.

Dominic reached for her hand, covering her cold fingers with his warmth. "What's wrong?"

"He found out about us."

Dominic's grip tightened on her hand. "It's all right."

She pulled her hand back. "No. It isn't. Now he'll never take me seriously. He'll think I'm sleeping with all of my clients. He'll think that's how I get them to sign with me." A tear fell down her cheek. "By sleeping with them."

"He knows you'd never do that."

She blinked away tears. "You didn't."

A spark of anger lit Dominic's eyes. "You know that I'm sorry for thinking you wanted to be with JP. I was jealous. I should have known better. And I'm retiring because it's time for me to retire, not because I want so desperately to help you that I'm giving JP my spot. JP should play for the Outlaws because he's got the talent and they're the best team for him. Period."

She didn't know what to say. What to do. She didn't want him to be angry at her. Didn't he know how much she loved him? How much she'd always loved him?

"I know I've screwed up countless times," he continued in a raw voice. "I didn't recognize real love when it was right in front of me the whole time. I didn't see the real, amazing woman you are—but I'm not blind anymore."

Melissa's brain shouted the words *I love you* but she couldn't get her mouth to say them. Something inside her, some wounded part of her that had more questions than answers, held the words back.

∗

Dominic hated to watch her leave. He desperately wanted to fix everything. He wanted to call her father, tell him that *he* seduced Melissa, not the other way around. He wanted to pull Melissa into his arms and kiss her until she saw reason. He wanted to be there for her emotionally and professionally, to assist her in the exhausting work of managing a player like JP.

But he couldn't do any of those things. Not if he wanted there to be a snowball's chance in hell for Melissa to realize that he could change, that he could back off and let her take the wheel.

And that she loved him, too.

CHAPTER TWENTY-SEVEN

As she drove down the winding freeway to San Francisco, Melissa felt thirteen years old again, terrified about bringing home a B on her report card, praying that her father never found out about the one and only biology class she'd ever skipped—but knowing that he would—and that she'd be grounded for a month for the transgression.

Fortunately, the four-hour drive gave her plenty of time to think. Time to realize that she no longer needed his praise to feel good about herself.

Somewhere during the past week, she'd turned a corner. Partly because of Dominic, but mostly because she'd finally started to value her own worth, she had finally looked up and realized that she was capable of doing amazing things, both professionally and per-sonally.

From here on out, she was going to live her life on

her own terms. She was going to figure out what she wanted, and then she was going to go out and get it.

The only question that remained was what to do about Dominic. She loved him, yet the chasm between them was wider than ever.

✳

The next morning, Melissa walked into her father's office at eight o'clock sharp. His face looked like thunder.

"You have betrayed me and you have betrayed my agency with your thoughtless actions. I can hardly stand to look at you."

She stood her ground. "I'm not a kid anymore. I can date whomever I want and I can love whomever I want."

"My players are off-limits. If Dominic leaves my agency, it'll be your fault."

"I understand your concern. And that's why I've already severed the relationship."

He looked surprised, but still furious. "You should never have gotten involved with him. Never."

She nodded. "You're right. I shouldn't have, but not for the reason you think. I made the mistake of falling in love with one of the best men I've ever known. Unfortunately, he's not the right guy for me. One day, I hope I can forgive you for putting money above your own daughter's happiness."

His mouth opened, then shut. By his silence, she knew how deeply she'd hurt him with her accusation. She turned to leave his office, then realized she'd left out one very important thing.

"I quit."

She walked out and rode down the elevator with her head held high. All her life she'd wanted her father's approval, an outward display of his love. Now, even though she knew she'd done the right thing, the divide between them was too deep. Her hopes for a stronger relationship with her father could never come to pass.

She checked her voice mail, and the sound of Dominic's voice sent chills up her spine. He had set up a meeting for JP with the Outlaws' general manager.

God, how she wanted to call him and confide all her fears and doubts to him. She wanted him to hold her in his arms and tell her that he loved her, that everything was going to be okay.

She was also worried about him. He was probably sitting down with the reporter from the *San Francisco Chronicle* right now, telling him everything. It was going to be a big story; there was no way around that. She desperately wanted to be there for him, holding his hand, letting him know that he was loved and lovable, no matter what mistakes he'd made as an adolescent.

By the time she met JP in front of the Outlaws' headquarters, she had a raging headache.

"I take it things didn't work out between you and Dom?" he said when he looked at her.

What was the point of denying everything? Dominic was brave enough to face his dirty laundry. She'd face up to hers.

"No. They didn't."

JP shook his head. "That sad sack of shit. I was sure he was going to tell you he loved you."

She chewed the inside of her lip. "He did."

JP looked at her like she was a crazy woman. "I truly don't get women. At least think about giving him a chance, okay? I know he's old and beaten up, but he's a pretty good guy underneath."

She took a deep breath. "Forget my love life. It's time to focus on football. Here's the deal: You shouldn't even have this chance. Any other player would have been filling out applications for a real job by now."

JP held up his hands to fend her off. "Trust me, boss, I know. Dominic's already read me the riot act for three days."

Her gaze was steady. "I don't know what lucky star you were born under, but having Dominic swoop in and turn you into a decent player, and then decide to retire so you have a shot at his spot, is pretty much the luckiest thing I've ever seen." She paused to make sure he understood what she was saying. "Don't blow it today. One fumble, one misstep, and everything comes crashing down. Got it?"

JP nodded respectfully. "Loud and clear. Now let's go kick some ass."

*

By that afternoon, her phones wouldn't stop ringing. The *San Francisco Chronicle* had printed an interview with Dominic about not only his past but his role in training JP. Word quickly hit the street that the Outlaws were thinking about signing him to their already full roster.

Other teams knew what this meant. A guy like Dominic DiMarco wouldn't put his reputation behind anyone who didn't have the elusive "it" that won Super Bowl rings.

Melissa had spent several years assisting her father during free-agent negotiations and she knew exactly how this game worked. The only problem was, she didn't have enough hands to take care of everything, enough phones or space in her voice mail to deal with the messages. A stack of thirty unanswered voice mails sat on her kitchen table. What she wouldn't give for an assistant.

Even though she should have been concentrating solely on JP's career, Melissa couldn't help thinking about Dominic. Had there been any backlash from the article? Was Dominic feeling vulnerable? Did he have anyone to lean on?

More than anything, she wanted to comfort him, confess her love.

But she couldn't. If she kissed him, touched him, they'd just keep playing out the same scene again and again.

Him helping her. Her resenting it.

Him declaring his love. Her not sure she believed it, with mind-blowing sex to fill in any gaps. Sex that only confused her more.

Her phone stopped ringing and in the rare silence a glimmer of realization took shape. She'd always assumed that Dominic had helped her because he didn't think she was strong enough or talented enough to handle the business on her own. But what if she'd been wrong?

When they'd worked with JP at his lakefront house, Dominic hadn't once questioned her judgment. He'd looked at her with respect, agreed with her decisions pertaining to JP's career.

Could it be that he'd helped her because he was a good man who loved her and only wanted what was best for her?

Both phones rang at the same time. Right now, business had to come first. As soon as JP's new deal was put to rest, she'd turn her entire focus to her relationship with Dominic.

CHAPTER TWENTY-EIGHT

The following morning, Melissa's first stop was JP's house. She'd kept him abreast of negotiations throughout the previous day, and as of seven a.m. he was officially a San Francisco Outlaw.

Holding a bottle of champagne in the crook of her arm, she rang the doorbell. A woman yelled, "Coming," from behind the closed door.

The woman's voice was strangely familiar, but when her friend Alice opened the door wearing nothing but one of JP's T-shirts, Melissa couldn't contain her shocked expression.

"What? How?"

Alice dragged her inside, then inspected the label on the champagne bottle.

"You have excellent taste," she proclaimed. "This is going to be yummy."

"You? JP?" Melissa was reduced to stuttering. "I don't get it."

Alice shook her head. "Me, neither. All I know is that he's funny. I've never dated a guy with a sense of humor before."

Her friend's face and eyes looked softer than Melissa remembered having seen them, and she was glowing. Amazing.

Alice leaned in close and said in a stage whisper, "And he's seriously talented in the bedroom."

Melissa held up a hand. "I don't think I can handle the details."

"I never in a million years thought I'd be having hot monkey sex with a pro football player. And that I'd like it. I thought you might not exactly approve."

Alice's words tugged at her heart. "I want you to be happy. And if JP makes you happy, then I'm happy. I'm just surprised. That's all." She pulled her friend into a hug. "You could have called and warned me, though," she teased.

"I feel really bad about not returning your phone calls. I was embarrassed at first."

JP walked into the kitchen wearing boxer shorts. "I heard that," he said to Alice, grabbing her and kissing her.

Judging by their kiss, he wasn't the least bit upset by what Alice had said about him. Maybe he wasn't cocky. Maybe he was just surprisingly secure, when all the rest of them were emotional basket cases.

"Hey, boss," he finally said. "Thanks for the killer new deal."

Still reeling, Melissa said, "Congratulations. Now don't fuck it up."

"I won't let him," Alice said with a wicked gleam in her eyes. JP pulled her into his arms and Melissa smiled at them, knowing she was already forgotten.

Maybe, she suddenly thought, *love doesn't always have to make sense.*

* * *

Fifteen minutes later, Melissa stepped out of a taxi in front of the McKnight Agency building. Sunbeams peeked through the tall buildings as she stood on the sidewalk and looked at the familiar scene. Businesspeople rushed to work in suits and heels; a few women chatted in front of the corner coffee shop with babies in front-packs on their chests.

Everything was just as it had always been.

And yet completely different.

When she stepped into the McKnight Agency foyer, she was immediately surrounded by people shaking her hand, all talking at once. Clearly, no one knew about her scene with her father yesterday. No one seemed to know that she'd quit and walked out.

"Congratulations!"

"You've made the deal of the year."

"How'd you turn JP around so quickly?"

"I learned everything I know from you guys," she said with a wide grin.

A few minutes later, she faced the long walk to her father's office. He must have heard the commotion, but he hadn't come out to greet her. After the way she'd left his office, throwing the words *I quit* at him, it was up to her to make the first move.

Just like she'd need to make the first move with Dominic.

Angie was at her usual post in front of Tom's office, a rare smile on her face. "We're all so proud of you," she said softly.

In all the years they'd known each other, this was the nicest and most personal thing Angie had ever said to her.

"Go on in," Angie said. "Your father's waiting for you. And, honey"—she paused, which gave Melissa a moment to digest the very unexpected endearment— "go easy on him."

Melissa opened the door. Her father immediately stood up. Strangely, he looked nervous.

"Congratulations," he said before she could close the door. "I'm very impressed with the deal you negotiated for JP."

She swallowed back sudden tears. "All my life," she admitted, "I've wanted you to be proud of me."

"I already was," he said, with a shake of his head. "But I never knew how to tell you." He cleared his throat. "I didn't mean what I said about you and Dominic—the way I said it."

"I know you didn't, Daddy. Our relationship shouldn't have been a secret."

"You couldn't have chosen a better man."

"I know."

The next thing she knew, his arms were around her and he was hugging her, just like he used to when she was little and had skinned her knee. He'd always loved her. Now it felt good to know that he respected her, as well.

Many moments later, she bit her lip. "Speaking of Dominic, I was hoping I could ask for the advice of the top agent in the business?"

Pleasure lit her father's eyes. "If you mean me, of course."

They sat on the couch. "I can't represent Dominic and be in a relationship with him, too."

"But I thought you said you weren't seeing each other anymore?" Her father actually looked hopeful at the thought of things working out between her and Dominic.

She shook her head. "We're not. But I've been thinking a lot about things. I want to try to work things out."

Her father squeezed her hand. "Your mother and I are there for you. Anytime. For any reason."

Something warm and solid bloomed in her

chest and she nodded, unable to speak. Finally, she turned the focus back to Dominic's career. "So—any great agents you can recommend for my star player? Someone who has experience with great players? Who knows the business better than anyone else?"

"Are you saying you'd like me to work with him again?" her father asked.

She nodded and her father beamed with pleasure. "I can only accept if you'll consider rejoining the agency."

She hugged him again. "Thank you. For everything."

CHAPTER TWENTY-NINE

Fifteen minutes later, Melissa stood silently in Dominic's hallway. A little more than a week ago, he had carried her over his shoulder out of a bar and into his life. But she'd been so full of hopes and dreams and insecurities that she'd turned her back on the love of the greatest man she'd ever known.

And then Dominic had told her his painful story and she'd finally realized that neither of them was perfect.

They didn't need to be perfect. The situation didn't need to be perfect.

All that mattered was the way they felt about each other.

She rang the doorbell, finally understanding what it meant to have one's heart in one's hands. Her arms trembled and so did her legs. But this time, she wasn't going to run. She was going to face her fears one by one until she'd conquered them all. She was going to look Dominic straight in the eye and tell him she loved him.

Dominic opened the door and she stood just looking at him, mesmerized by his beauty, his grace.

"May I come in?"

He moved aside to let her in and she could barely wait for the door to click shut. "I came here to tell you . . ." The words caught in her throat.

Dominic took her hands, and his touch was so strong, so warm. "Go ahead," he said softly. "I'm listening."

She looked up into his eyes, praying her words would come out right. "I've been in love with you for a long time, Dominic. As long as I can remember."

He smiled. "I know."

"I thought you never noticed me," she said softly. "You were so much older, so much more experienced. I never thought you'd look at me like this, never thought you'd hold me."

"You always were a sweet kid," he agreed, "until you weren't a kid anymore."

"But I wasn't your type," she protested.

"I made sure of that," he replied. "How do you think I felt, lusting after my agent's daughter? You were legal, but that didn't mean you weren't off-limits." He closed the space between them one inch at a time. "But that's not why I pushed you away."

"Then why?" she whispered.

He pulled her against him and lowered his mouth, capturing her lips in a kiss that left her breathless. "You make me feel things I never wanted to feel again." His voice was rough with emotion. "When I'm with you, I lose control. Over my body. My mind." He found her mouth again and warmth spread through her body from her head to her toes. "Especially my heart."

"I do, too," she admitted, "but it's different than how I imagined. Better, because it's real. *You're* real. I'd spent so many years dreaming of you, but the truth is, until this week I hardly knew you at all."

"And now that you know everything, have your feelings changed?"

"They have," she said softly. "Because your wild teenage years, the bad things you've done, the innate power you work so hard to control, the way you make decisions for people whether they like it or not—all of that makes you the man I love today . . . and the man I'll love forever."

He picked her up and carried her down the hall to his bedroom. "For twenty years, I've punished myself for what I did when I was in high school. I've kept my distance from everyone, especially you— because I knew I could love you. I knew I wanted to have a home with you, children with you, the rest of my life with you." He captured her mouth in another hot kiss. "But I can't live without you, so I'm going to have to learn to live with myself and my past."

"I've never loved you properly," he murmured as he laid her down on his bed.

She sank into the soft down duvet. "Yes, you have. Every time."

Dominic pulled his Outlaws T-shirt up over his head. The sight of his bare chest, his tanned skin and rippling muscles, took her breath away, just as it always had.

Just as it always would.

"Am I ever going to get used to looking at you?" she asked with a smile.

Dominic's eyes were hot as he gazed down at her. "I've been asking myself the same question about you."

And Melissa truly felt like the most beautiful woman in the world.

He dropped his jeans to the floor, and as she lay against plush pillows, she allowed herself to fully appreciate the gorgeous man who had just offered her his heart.

And then he was moving to her, nearly naked in blue boxer shorts, and she reached for him, pulling all 230 pounds of gorgeous male down onto the bed, loving the moment when the hard planes of his body covered her, his heat penetrating her clothes, his erection pressing into her thigh. His

lips found hers and he was so gentle, so tender, until he wasn't anymore. Before she knew it, her clothes were beside his on the floor, and her arms were wrapped around his broad shoulders, her legs around his waist, and he was moving inside her. They stayed like that for a long moment, just holding each other, Dominic's heartbeat throbbing against Melissa's.

"I love you," she whispered against his lips, knowing she'd never tire of telling him with words, and with her body, how much she loved every part of him.

It had taken her a long time to understand that love was complicated, and that that was okay. She loved her father, even though he'd always had the power to hurt her deeply, and she knew he loved her, too, in his own complex way. She loved her job, even though it was often difficult and frustrating. She'd even learned to love herself, to look past her faults and insecurities to the strong, intelligent woman she'd always been on the inside.

Most of all, she loved Dominic, both for the good deeds he'd done and for everything he was ashamed of. His strong conscience was just one of the things she loved about him. He believed in justice, even if he was on the losing end. Together they'd find other ways to keep kids out of trouble through sports.

Fortunately, Melissa knew exactly how to keep

Dominic out of trouble . . . by keeping him in bed.
With her. For as long as possible.

"I can't get enough of you," he said, and she
remembered his saying those same words to her the
first time they'd made love. Only now, after he took
her to the peaks of ecstasy, after he'd exploded and
cried out her name, he added, "I love you, Melissa. I
always will."

After they caught their breath, he smiled into her
eyes. "We need to talk about one more thing." Glori-
ously naked, he got out of bed and scooped her up in
his arms.

"Where are you taking me?" she asked.

"To where it all began."

He carried her into the living room and released
her so that she slid down his body. He knelt before
her, just as he had that first night.

But this time he held out a black velvet box. Every
last one of her dreams was coming true.

"Melissa, will you marry me?"

Dropping to her knees, she put her hands on his
cheeks and pulled him on top of her. "Much better,"
she said.

Smiling eyes looked down at her, even as his
cock rose against her belly. "Now are you ready to
answer me?"

She smiled back. "Yes, Dominic, I'll marry you."
Rolling over so that she was on top, she slid onto him

one delicious inch at a time. "And I can't think of any better way to seal the deal."

*

The following Saturday, the guests at Dominic's annual summer party at Lake Tahoe agreed that it was his best yet. Any surprise at his relationship with Melissa McKnight quickly gave way to the obvious love between them.

Dominic and Melissa stood in the center of the yard and asked for everyone's attention.

"I'd like to thank everyone for making the drive up Highway Fifty another year," Dominic said. "Since everyone's here, I figure this is the perfect time to announce that this will be my final season with the Outlaws."

Shock rippled through the crowd and Melissa reached for Dominic's hand in support.

"Fortunately, I won't be leaving the game I love so much. Instead I'll be sharing an office with Melissa McKnight. She's going to take care of the deals, while I work with the players to take their skills to the highest level possible." He grinned. "If you know any great players who are under the radar, let us know. We'll whip them into shape."

*

Three months later in the very same spot, four dozen Outlaws cheered and whistled, and everyone agreed that their wedding was the good-luck charm the team needed to make it to the Super Bowl one more time.

＊

When the Outlaws did win again, Melissa often left her wedding rings at home in favor of her Super Bowl ring.